The Eight of Swords

By Petra Kidd

When you come home to your world turned upside down, what might the future hold?

For Dilys, my mother, my friend

Cover Design by MyriadLifeBooks

1.

People often recall what they were doing, where they were, who they were with, and how old they were when a major event occurs. For many years to come, they will say, "Oh yes, when the planes hit the towers, I had just arrived in Cuba for my first holiday in two years," or "When the Queen Mother's death was announced, the entire family was here for lunch, including Aunty Martha, whom we hadn't seen since Uncle Stephen passed away." All the minor details of the moment they learnt about a terrible or significant event flood their memories.

The same holds true for more intimate events. These are events that, while occurring in the present moment, continue to permeate our thoughts and memories for a lifetime. On the day I returned home and my key refused to turn in the lock, the news of a colleague's tragic suicide by jumping in front of a tube train during rush hour consumed my mind. I can't tell you that I had any gut feeling or intuition that this day would become such a significant turning point in my life. The day began as any other; my alarm sounded, I activated the ten-minute snooze feature, tightly closed my eyes, and hoped that each minute would transform into an hour. Of course such an outcome is impossible, but when you hate your work, every little delay in getting there becomes a mini freedom.

I can even remember the dream I had before I woke up. It involved a tea party in the middle of a field with buttercups and dandelions. A voice said, "Don't pick the dandelions, or you will wee in your bed'. I often wonder if that somehow signalled the events of the day, and why, if it did, I got such a pointless and unhelpful warning.

I stood on the doorstep for a full ten minutes before realising that my key did not fit this lock. I scanned the front of the house to make sure that in my confused and distracted state I hadn't mistaken someone else's house for my own, but no, it was indeed my house: the door remained red with a brass knocker in the shape of a mermaid, weeds had grown over the air vent, and rain dripped in a reluctant waterfall from the guttering. No, this was definitely my abode of the past eight years, the place I bought after my second divorce, vowing I would never again share my home, my heart, and my possessions with another person.

Stepping back I glanced at my watch; I don't know why. Every evening I walked home from work, setting out from my office around sixish, whatever the weather, regardless of the time of year. I trudged through snow, battled wind, rain, and hail, slid around on ice, squinted through fog, and wore a ridiculously large hat to keep the rarely sighted sun of recent summers off my pale-skinned face. Somehow, I seemed to think the time might give me an answer as to why my key wouldn't fit the lock. Then, I glimpsed the curtain briefly twitching open. The curtain fell back into place immediately.

Did I imagine that? Rainwater soaked my shoulders as I stood perplexed trying to make sense of the situation. I leant over and tapped on the window. Nothing happened. The curtain didn't move again. It occurred to me at this point that perhaps I should try using my backdoor key. I fumbled to pick it out among all the other keys on the ring—the keys to my desk drawers at work, the shed key, my elderly neighbour's key, and a bicycle lock key I had stopped using many moons ago.

I began to walk around the right side of the house—across the tiny front garden, through the side gate, and along the muddy path to the back door. Again I inserted the key into the lock and tried to turn it, and it did not budge. I managed to stop myself from hammering on the frosted glass window of the door. How ridiculous would that be? Knocking on my door to be let into the house where only I lived. On examination, the lock looked shinier than my normal rusty-edged lock —brand new, in fact. My heart jigged a little in a downward way, my legs weakened, and my stomach did a backflip; panic had finally set in.

I put the keys in my coat pocket and walked slowly back to the front of the house, pondering the situation. Back at the front door, I grasped the mermaid knocker firmly, thumping it three times against the door. Nothing happened. I inspected the lock; again, it appeared to be shiny and new. A couple of deep scratches and a dent I didn't recognise were next to them.

Someone had changed the locks.

I simply didn't know what to do. Bizarrely the thought ran through my mind that somehow my colleague had faked his death, come around, broken into my house and locked me out. Why would he do that? We hadn't been particularly friendly— or not friendly. For the past year since his appointment to my team, we exchanged personal pleasantries on an irregular basis, shared a filing cabinet, made each other the odd cup of tea, and displayed only cursory interest in one another beyond our work. A burglar wouldn't have changed the locks. None of my family would play such a prank. My parents lived abroad. My brother, a well-off stockbroker, lived happily in Surrey with his wife and two children. The only members of my extended family were an elderly aunt and a spinster cousin who lived in Australia. Friends and acquaintances were not of the type to do this either; they were, for the most part, professionals, reasonably well off, and fully encompassed in their own complicated lives—far too busy and harassed to decide to break into my house, change the locks, and then refuse to open the door. They weren't the kind of people who would think such an elaborate prank funny.

My mind skidded round a very short track and passed the finish line in a matter of seconds without any sensible conclusion.

I woke up and noticed a light was on in my bedroom. Suddenly, anger replaced the panic. What the hell was going on? I slammed the knocker down as hard as I could, causing the door to shake with the force. I pummelled the wood with my fist, knuckles stinging with effort.

Without warning, the door flew open, and I would have fallen straight into the hallway had not a large, black-haired man been standing there, filling the doorway with his extraordinarily wide shoulders. I stepped back in shock, clutched my handbag to my chest and gasped, "What?" I should have said other words, such as "Who?" Why? How?" But my mouth gaped open silently, leaving only the sound of my ragged breath in the early evening air.

The man's top lip curled up and spread into a kind of amused snarl. "What you wan'?"

For the second time, I wondered if my bewildered brain had brought me home to the wrong house. Once again, I double-checked the mermaid, the weeds, and the air vent. "I live here!" My voice sounded shrill, as if I disbelieved my own declaration.

"Oh?" He said this in a questioning manner, and for a moment I badly wanted to punch his leering face, but given his height and width, I immediately thought better of it. I half expected him to follow the 'oh' with, 'So that's what *you* think?' IInstead, he pushed the door open wider, revealing a woman with long black plaits on either side of her plump face and a mosaic of other faces peering around her body at me.

Had I somehow received a bang on the head and lost consciousness? Surely I had forgotten something – how, for instance, had this family of strangers come to be gathered in my house? Perhaps during my job as an immigration official, I had unwittingly invited these people to live here. Suggested they pop round, change the locks and make themselves at home. A clone of me had acted on a subconscious whim. It's true; I often felt sympathy for people I had to send back to the country they had come from, often war-torn or suffering some horrific disaster or a cruel dictatorship because of their lack of visas or work permits. No obvious explanation dropped out of the sky, so I stood rooted to the spot, incredulous, clutching my handbag as if my life depended on it. They had taken my house; perhaps at any moment they would reach out for the only possession I apparently still had hold of.

The man waved his hand graciously to beckon me in. Beckon me in to my own hall.

"I am going to call the police." I stated this uncertainly and not remotely as emphatically as I should have.

The man tilted back his head and chuckled with amusement. "No, please, come in."

The woman, unsmiling, nodded at me and made way for me to enter.

So I did.

2.

On entry to my house, I could see I hadn't made any mistake. I strode past my embroidered animal pictures, inherited from my dexterous grandmother. A few paces took me into the sitting room, where the wall had been knocked through before I bought the house to reveal a small but wide-windowed dining room. Three figures sat at my oak-carved circular dining table; chairs had been moved from the lounge to accommodate more people. A large hairy dog had taken up residence on my Persian rug, a present from my brother during his travels as a student. It briefly glanced up at me with disinterest before continuing to lick its hindquarters with a huge pink tongue.

Speechless just about sums up my feelings; I am not sure at which point I clamped my mouth shut in consternation. It could have been as an elderly woman with a mouth as small and wrinkled as an anus raised a crystal glass from a set of four I'd bought in House of Fraser during a moment of rash indulgence and murmured what could have been a damning spell at me. Or it might have been when the small child near the fireplace lifted my father's prized cricket bat and whacked the dinner gong my second husband bought as a joke. They are not exactly the most important factors in the rude, uninvited occupation of my hard-earned home but stand out in my memory as clearly as if they were happening at this very moment.

I sank into a chair and gazed at the scene before me. My vintage 1920s lamp cast an amber glow across the room, leaving much of it in shadow. My house was filled with people of all ages, from young to old. It reminded me of actors on a stage, all ready to perform.

The man, who'd answered my own front door and let me in, appeared in front of me. His face leaned forward into mine, chunky, ringed fingers spread across his knees. "You wan' a drink?"

I nodded, paralysed by incredulity. Within moments, the crone at the table had filled a tumbler with red wine and passed it to the man, who pressed it firmly into my hand. "Drink!" He gave the order as if he were a jovial host.

I took a long gulp, then another.

"So what do you wan'?" Hands withdrawn to hips, the man gazed quizzically at me.

Unable to form words, I took another gulp of wine.

"You wan' something?"

I knew I should shout at them all to get out. I knew I should get angry and assert myself, but despite my initial fury and confusion, perhaps placated by the wine, I couldn't help but find the situation ridiculously amusing. Laughter burst out of me like an exploding bubble, spittle flying through the air.

The broad-shouldered man grinned, but the hard, cold penetration of his eyes sobered my hilarity almost as soon as it had begun.

"So what you wan'?"

"I live here! This is my house, my home!" I took another gulp of wine; my hand shook a little. I thought about standing up but wasn't sure my legs would stand firm beneath me after such a shock. "The question is not what I want but what the heck you lot are doing here?"

The man drew himself upright, squared his shoulders, and fixed me with a deadly serious glare. "No, no, you not live here!" He emphasised "here" to accentuate his point, sweeping a large, knuckled hand across the room. "This belongs to nobody, where we live." He enunciated the words loudly and carefully, as if making sure I understood. Then he moved towards me and squatted down. "You", he jabbed a finger at my chest, "are OUR guest!"

This had started to feel like an odd game of bluff. At what point would I wake up, or would one of these people suddenly shout "gotcha"? As if I had fallen for their little joke. Or a big elaborate joke that involved several actors and the expense of changed locks. I sat and tried to make sense of it all in my befuddled head. I took another gulp of wine and then held out my glass for more.

The crone with the anal mouth lifted the bottle in acknowledgement as if to say, "You want more?" Come and get it. Unable to move, I handed the glass to the black-haired man, who obediently walked over to pour more wine. My noisy kitchen clock chimed seven o'clock. I couldn't believe I had been here for half an hour; I hadn't called the police or even asked for help from anyone, and I sat surrounded by strangers in my own home. Then I realised I could smell food being cooked. Surely I would wake up in a minute and press the snooze option. After all, I needed to find out what would happen next in this strange dream.

As the man handed me back the newly filled glass, he nodded, "I am Yan. I mus' introduce my family to you. I forget my manners." He beckoned to the woman with the plaited hair and plump face, "Vadoma." She stared at me, and I stared back, unsure of how to respond. Eventually, I nodded. Yan then waved his hand toward the elderly woman who had poured my wine into one of my glasses at my dining room table. "Bunica". I raised my glass in greeting, and she parted her lips to reveal a cavernous black hole. Then he gestured to the boy who had whacked the gong with my father's cricket bat. "Bo." I gave Bo the best forbidding stare I could muster.

Two girls and a boy sat over near the window. Yan pointed at them, "Florica, Lala, Hanzi, my children." He clicked his fingers, and the dog looked up. "Boldo, our dog." He grinned triumphantly, and the dog stuck out its tongue as if to goad me further.

How could I call the police now? By some weird illusion I had become the guest of what I realised were Romanian gypsies. I had come into brief contact with one or two in my time as an immigration official, but I knew next to nothing of their customs, history, or culture. I had lost all sense of reasoning due to tiredness, the emotion of the day, and drinking red wine a little too quickly. "I'm Jayne." I muttered into my glass.

Yan gestured at a pile of envelopes on the sideboard, "Mrs Jayne Patchett".

Occasionally, I used to create scenarios in my mind and imagine how I would react. For instance, what would happen if I found myself in a car accident? Could my limited first aid training suffice to save a life? What if my neighbour found himself trapped in the bathtub and requested my assistance? What if a plane crashed in the next street? Crazy happenings, like if someone knocked on the door having just been mugged. Would I trust them and call for help, or would I turn them away in case they were scamming me? I experimented with fleeting ideas to test what my action plan might be. Never in all my daydreams, could I have imagined returning from work to discover a group of Romanian gypsies in my house, seemingly without having caused any damage to a window to gain entry, consuming my wine, and using whatever they found in the fridge to prepare meals. To make matters worse, this Yan character now told me I was a guest in my own sitting room while his elderly mother, or perhaps mother-in-law, poured me wine.

I sighed heavily, placed my wine glass on the floor next to my chair, rested my head in my hands, squeezed my eyes tightly shut, and hoped the bizarre scene I had come home to witness might somehow magically evaporate. The alarm would buzz, and I could tell my friends, perhaps even my doctor, of how ridiculous and realistic my dreams had become lately, a menopausal blip of some kind.

3.

Yan paced my sitting room floor, large scuffed fingers gripping his belt, which I noticed had a rather unusual buckle. I couldn't make out the emblem on it, but it appeared to be a Cloisonné design. I recognised this style because an old school friend I still kept in touch with collected Cloisonné pieces.

He cocked his head to one side and glared in my direction as if trying to intimidate me into leaving.

The children murmured among themselves as they fiddled with my ornaments. Out of the corner of my eye I saw the boy, Hanzi, pick up a pewter goblet I didn't have much regard for and pretend to drink from it.

If Yan had been there alone, I would never have entered the house. His eyebrows spread thickly above his dark, menacing eyes. His bulbous nose, thick lips, and square shoulders exuded power and control. I knew I had to choose my words and actions carefully to have any hope of winning this standoff. It seemed unlikely that he would forcefully remove me from the house with his family watching, but who could tell? Perhaps my middle-class belief in the niceties of life was in conflict with the stark realities. For all I had seen in the course of my professional life, I still managed to maintain a certain naivety at times.

I could hear pans clang against one another in my kitchen. The aroma of the lamb I had stored in the freezer for my Sunday lunch wafted through the doorway, tantalising my nostrils. My stomach churned with hunger; my last meal, a limp tuna and cucumber sandwich, was now a long-distant memory.

Absently I wondered if these people would ever leave. My silence seemed unsettling for Yan, but the others apparently accepted my presence with little interest. Only the old crone fixed her rheumy eyes upon me as if waiting for the glass in my hand to empty again.

"So, you wan' eat with us?"

I stifled a laugh. "Well, yes, that is kind of you. I am hungry after working all day." I emphasised the word "working," probably because I saw these people as not working but just taking, and at this precise moment, they were taking from me. I wondered what Yan might be thinking. The deeply burrowed line between his eyebrows lengthened in an exaggerated frown.

Yan leant his arm against the wall a moment, surveyed the dining table and growled instructions in Romanian to Hanzi, which included the word 'femeile', obviously referring to the women in the room. He gestured for me to come to the table. Propelled by hunger and mellowed by wine, I obediently stood up and moved towards it. The elderly crone shifted her long skirt to accommodate my legs. A mixture of my best china and pieces I kept for everyday use had been carefully laid out. Hanzi rummaged through the drawers for cutlery, grabbed a handful, and noisily flung it onto a plate.

My mobile phone began to ring. It rang loudly and vibrated as if trying to release itself from my handbag. I didn't move; instead, I stared at Yan. What was I waiting for, permission to answer?

As if we were playing statues, everyone froze. A girl with long dark hair emerged from the kitchen carrying my casserole dish, wearing my oven gloves and apparently an old summer skirt of mine.

It was as if Snow White had arrived. I half expected seven dwarves to trip along behind her carrying condiments.

Yan gestured for her to place the dish in front of the old crone. The noise from my phone ceased, and I fought the urge to check who'd rung. Occasionally there were emergency work calls in the evening. This new situation relieved me of normal stresses, and bizarrely, although I couldn't exactly say I was enjoying myself, I felt compelled to see what would happen next. Relinquishing control came with a strange kind of relief.

Vadoma, his wife, strode in carrying a tray of roasted vegetables. It all smelt delicious. Placing the tray in the centre of the dining table, she returned to the kitchen, only to reappear moments later carrying a tray of freshly baked bread.

They sat and ate, occasionally exchanging surreptitious glances. Yan placed both hands on the table. "You heard Bulibasha?"

I shook my head, expecting to be told this was a traditional Roman gypsy song and half looking forward to hearing it. Evidently, the wine had permeated my mind, leading me to view this invasion of my personal space as a form of entertainment.

"Well, this no you house, this no my house, this not anybody's house!" Delighted with this declaration, he sat back in his chair and thumped his fist on the table, rattling the china. "We take what we wan'." He pushed his bulbous nose almost within touching distance of my own. "Is no yours."

His arrogance angered me.

"I say, I leader. Bulibasha."

Heads nodded around the table.

Choking down a lump of meat, I jabbed a finger in his direction. "This is *my* house; you are all eating *my* food from *my* table. I should have called the police and had you all turfed out immediately, but…"

Why hadn't I simply stayed on the doorstep, called the police, and had them throw out these lawless squatters?

Throughout my working life, I'd witnessed families torn apart and individuals being sent back to countries where they would live in fear for their lives, struggle to find employment, and fail to achieve any meaningful life. I'd seen people incarcerated purely for trying to seek a better, safer life; why should I be secure, well-fed, and reside so comfortably when they had nothing?

My head spun.

How stupid was I? This family, firmly ensconced at my dining table, certainly didn't appear destitute; in fact, Yan had a finely formed round belly. Although his shirt bore signs of wear mended with neat stitching, his fingers boasted heavy gold rings, and around his neck lay a gold amulet on a chain. He wasn't the one paying the mortgage and bills here; he hadn't spent half an hour deliberating in the supermarket over which joint of meat to buy, and he didn't have to work all day with irritable people (even suicidal in one case).

My left eyelid twitched in annoyance.

"You really have no right!" My voice squeaked in fury, but I sounded like a trapped sparrow, not a raging homeowner usurped by cuckoos.

Vadoma sat down next to me, her elbow clumsily knocking mine. Yan ignored me and carried on eating. Hanzi sat on the floor feeding lumps of bread to Boldo, and the girls sullenly fiddled with their hair. A young man who had appeared when Snow White brought the food in was sitting by the television, examining the remote control.

Where were all these people going to sleep? My head swam, my eyes were heavy, and I barely had the energy to think, let alone decide what to do.

Yan, apparently content with his meal, drained his glass dry and pushed it at the elderly woman. She shook her head and pointed at the empty bottle. He rose from his chair and made his way towards the kitchen, presumably in search of more wine.

"You all need to leave; you can't remain here."

The room fell silent, except for Boldo, who was chewing noisily on what I realised was the remaining lamb bone.

"I would rather not call the police, but I will have to. This is my home. You seem like nice enough people, but the law is the law."

Yan's voice rumbled into my ear like a ten-tonne truck pulling up: "What law? We respect no law!"

Snow White turned beautiful pleading eyes my way, her fright obvious.

"The law of this country is that you can't just go entering people's houses and making yourselves at home; it isn't legal."

My voice sounded weary but emphatic enough.

Hanzi looked up from wrestling Boldo on the rug. "But we like it here, lady. Can we stay here, Tată?"

Yan fixed his dark eyes on me while chiding Hanzi in words I could not understand.

As we stared one another down, I noticed the elderly woman squatting in the corner of my dining room. It took me a few moments to understand what this meant; I let out a weak squeal, but as I did so, it was already too late.

4.

I felt far more compelled to call the police after Bunica defecated in the corner of my dining room. Even Yan, while trying to defend the old lady from my verbal abuse, raised a sympathetic eyebrow as I scrubbed the floor with bleach. Hanzi and his sisters looked on sniggering, hands over their mouths.

Bunica shrugged as if to deny all responsibility.

Vadoma's mean mouth formed a rebellious line as she addressed me in nonsensical broken English. "She lady who old, she well not, you no shout at her that way!"

If Bunica had looked remotely ill or even slightly apologetic for her actions, I might have had a modicum of sympathy, but the sheer audacity rendered me furious.

"There are two bathrooms in this house, two!"

I spat the words at Vadoma and gestured toward Bunica, "I eat my meals in here and now I will be left with that image forever!"

"Have you no shame?" I pointlessly directed the question to Bunica, who sat, legs akimbo, gazing out of the window, murmuring to herself, oblivious of my fury.

Then I spotted that Bunica was wearing my tights, my new black patterned ones. I half wished I could give her a whack with my mop. I certainly wouldn't be wearing those should they come back into my possession. They weren't exactly cheap either, even from the supermarket.

These people really had to go.

Yan sat in my ex-husband's leather recliner fingering his way through a Lonely Planet guide to New Zealand bought just before he left me for his personal assistant, a loud-mouthed Kiwi with the scruples of Fagin. My handbag with the mobile phone in it lay on the floor right in front of him. I had two landline telephones, one in the hall and one in the bedroom. I knew I had no hope of using the hall phone, so I tried to think of an excuse to go upstairs to my bedroom. It occurred to me I shouldn't need to explain where I was going in my house, so I walked out of the room and stomped determinedly up the stairs.

No one came after me.

A strange smell lingered on the upstairs landing, making me hesitate to enter the bedroom. Fortunately, it didn't resemble excrement, but it certainly wasn't pleasant. A terrible case of body odour perhaps? It didn't surprise me after what had just happened downstairs. Various clothing and personal possessions, mostly mine, lay strewn around. I sighed at the thought of having to tidy them all away again.

The room lay in darkness, lit only by the outside street lamp. I could hear breathing. Surely there weren't more of them in here. I reached round and switched on the overhead light to be met with a thunderous snore and the sight of a grizzled-up face poking out from beneath my duvet. This I supposed might be Bunica's husband, with a matching anus-like mouth in a much larger and noisier version.

Undeterred, I moved around the bed, picking my way through the surrounding debris that had been turfed out from my wardrobe and drawers. The grizzled face turned to one side, snorted and continued sleeping. More expense, I thought; I'd have to buy new bed linen and another duvet. The man smelt as if he had been living in a compost heap for the past few weeks. Perhaps he had; who knew with this lot?

I found my phone hanging off the hook, picked it up, put the receiver to my ear and dialled 999. The operator took an age to answer. I could hear the family shifting around downstairs, their voices busily burbling beneath my feet. At any moment I expected Yan to appear in the doorway. Eventually a woman's voice asked me which service, "police". I replied, my voice shaking.

Explaining the details of my emergency as rapidly as I could, every word sounded fantastical: squatters, gypsies, my house, vandalism. A weird nightmare of non-imaginings. The voice at the other end repeated my address in a monotone voice as if this occurrence was nothing out of the ordinary. "Might be some time; they are very busy tonight; a football game is on, Arsenal and Chelsea, I think— no, Arsenal and Spurs." The voice paused and then went on, "They've not physically threatened you, have they?"

"Well, no, but…"

"You asked them to leave?"

At this point I became exasperated. "Well, of course I bloody have! Get someone here as fast as you can." I slammed down the receiver a little too hard, and the body in the bed grunted, opened one eye, then grasping the edge of the duvet, snottily blew his nose into it. I retched.

"Get out of my bed, get oooout!" I screeched wildly enough to shame a banshee, then vacated the room as fast as I could before I could be treated to any more horrible sights or sounds.

Downstairs, Yan sat examining my ornaments, rubbing his fingers over a cut crystal glass, then pinging it with his forefinger. Beside him lay a large holdall gradually being filled with items from my dresser.

"You can put those back where you found them; the police are on the way."

Yan shrugged. "What do you think they will do? We live here now." He jabbed a finger at me. "You rented it to us."

"I what?" I laughed, "In that case I look forward to seeing you show them the contract you signed."

"Verbal contract." Yan leered up at me as he popped silver napkin rings into his bag.

I snorted. "You sit there stealing my things and imagine that the police will take your crazy explanation for breaking and entering seriously!"

Vadoma appeared at my side, "Come, table; Bunica wan' tell you the future."

Her hand gripped my elbow. Did those words mean the old lady felt repentant for her defecation and wanted to make amends by telling me my fortune? Unbelievable. Whatever next? I could tell her about my future, where I would clear up the mess and ask the police to retrieve the objects her family were shamelessly pilfering. I hesitated for a moment, but seeing that Yan had no intention of stopping his careful selection of my household property anytime soon and that I didn't have the means to stop him myself, I followed Vadoma over to Bunica.

She sat rocking to and fro on her chair, eyes filmy, mouth drawn into a sucked-in pout. What could this aged crone possibly share with me that would be of interest?

Fascination overtook my fractured senses once again. Something told me I would almost miss this constant entertainment once the police had dragged them all away.

My existence up to this point can't exactly be described as lonely, as my daily life was locked into a routine of work, needlework, evening classes, theatre with friends, and the occasional awkward meal out with my brother and his family. In between times I read autobiographies of dead film stars and rugged folk who had the tenacity and desire to visit extreme places, risking their lives in a way totally alien to my mundane trip towards the final destination: the local cemetery.

Continuous activity dispelled any moments of self-pity or loneliness, but deep down in my soul, a pit of fear burned.

The children silently gathered around us, seemingly in awe of their grandmother. No giggles or muttering now.

Snow White's eyes grew round. Hanzi watched on as he absently stroked Boldo's ears. Even Boldo sat upright as if ready to take in every word the ancient crone might utter.

Suddenly she snapped the gnarled fingers of her right hand at Vadoma.

"Tarot Carti". She ordered.

Hanzi loudly sucked in his breath, but nobody looked his way, all eyes fixed on Bunica and me.

My heart gave a little hop; I'd never believed in such 'hogwash', but now I felt a certain thrill. This wasn't one of those people who featured in advertisements in the back of the newspaper or downmarket magazines, but a real-life genuine gypsy, who wore gold Creole hoop earrings and a head-square. Demented or not, I felt eager to hear what she might have to tell me.

Hopefully the police would be delayed.

5.

Our fortune-telling session ended with the tarot card Eight of Swords; Bunica's words were spilling forth via muddled translation from Vadoma when fierce hammering on the front door interrupted us.

My heart sank; how typical for the police to arrive when I was about to hear something crucial to my as yet unhopeful future.

Yan rose slowly from the recliner; beside it, his holdall lay fit to burst. He made no move to hide what he had shamelessly taken. His burly form disappeared into the hall, and I wondered if he would open the front door or ignore them.

When I heard the door open, I wasn't surprised. Given his earlier statements, he had no fear of them. I leant back in my chair, trying to see into the hallway, but my position didn't allow it.

The children stood transfixed, more by the card than the commotion at the front door. Only Hanzi's eyes darted fearfully from the table to the direction of raised voices.

I stood up; after all, I had called the police, so I should go and talk to them.

Reluctant as I felt to leave Bunica's strange ramblings, her occupation of my house, like that of the others, remained illegal, and even if I was keen to hear her predictions for my future, the immediate future would involve a court order and eviction of my newly acquired resident family.

Yan's frame filled the front doorway; two policemen stood outside, small and insignificant looking beneath his mighty form. I ducked beneath his left arm and out into the cold night air.

"Are you the owner of this property?" The younger-looking of the two directed the query to me.

Yan snorted, "She's our landlady."

I let out a sneering chortle. "I am not their landlady; I came home to find my locks changed and a whole family in here. They are total strangers to me."

Yan muttered the whole time I spoke, his eyes darting up and down the street, presumably checking if there were more police around. He yelled something back into the house, and moments later Hanzi appeared clutching a sheet of paper to his chest.

"What's that Hanzi?" I reached for the paper, but Yan snatched it away and handed it to the cop, who looked at it and then at me.

"So you know their names, then?" He raised his eyebrows at me. Surely he couldn't believe I was actually renting my property to them. If that was the case, why did he think I made a 999 call?

"What does it say?" I asked, ignoring the question.

"It appears to be some kind of property agreement between you, Mrs Jayne Patchett? And Mr Yanoro Dodrescu." He thrust it under my nose.

I caught a glimpse of curtains twitching across the road. Clearly, the neighbours had noticed the police car and were intrigued.

Sighing, I crumpled up the paper in my hand and said, "This is ridiculous; they obviously pulled a form off the Internet and filled it in."

"No know how to use a computer." Yan shrugged. "You gave it to us."

"He's lying; obviously he is lying. You should come in and see the mess they've made; he's filled holdalls with my stuff, and they've trashed the place. Come in, I'll show you!"

Yan and the officers stared at me. The older-looking policeman looked up at Yan. "Is it alright if we come in and take a look, sir?"

"Don't ask *him*!" I squealed in horror, "It's my bloody house; ask me!"

"Yes, but they're living here, so…"

"They are NOT *living* here. I came home to find the locks changed; I had to bang on the door to get into my own house."

"She comes to have drinks and a meal wi' us. Everything was fine; I don't understand why she got so upset." Yan's face contorted as if searching an internal dictionary for the words. "She is crazy." He made a circular motion with his fingertip next to his temple, then tugged his earlobe as if exasperated and mystified all at the same time. "We are good tenants."

The officer's eyes widened when he heard about the drink and meal; obviously he'd noticed my words slur a little. Now he eyed me suspiciously.

Even with a six-foot, thickset, blockbuster of a gypsy in front of him and all of these faces staring him in mock innocence, the stupid nappy-wearing copper couldn't see what was going on.

"We was having a nice time; Jayne here was just 'aving her fortune told by my, how do you say, in-law, Mamma? No understand why she calls you; she drinks too much."

Yan gave the policemen an elaborate wink. The older of the two grinned back at him.

So now we had Yan the comedian. I cursed my own stupidity in ever entering my own property and attempting to deal with the situation on my own.

"Have you got any witnesses to these people breaking into your property, Mrs Patchett?"

I glanced around the street; I couldn't disturb Hetty, my ninety-six-year-old arthritic neighbour, who would struggle to get up from her chair, and on the other side was a travelling salesman who had been overseas for the past month. The neighbours opposite, who had moved in recently, might have seen something; I hadn't met them yet. I strode over to their house and rang the doorbell, hoping they had seen something during their recent curtain twitching. By now it must have been nine o'clock; I could hear their television blasting out music; it sounded like an advertisement break. Eventually, a teenage boy, dressed as a Goth, cautiously opened the door a crack and grunted.

"Are your parents in? I need a word."

His eyes widened at the sight of the police car, and he slammed the door shut. When I rang the bell once more, a woman wearing a pink dressing gown flung it open.

"Sorry, love, Jamie thought they were here for him; he's been in a spot of bother at school. What's up? It looks like you've problems yourself." She moved forward to get a closer look at the policemen.

I explained the situation as best I could. It had been a tough day at work, what with the suicide and a whole host of other problems, and now all this—I suddenly felt exhausted. I half hoped she would invite me in for tea and sympathy.

Perhaps I could squat at her place until my squatters left.

"Not been here all day, but Gav might have seen something; he's my hubby; he's, er, on a break from work at the moment. Gav, Gav!"

After much grunting and muttering, Gav, the hubby, appeared. "Yes, love?"

"Squatters have invaded her house; they must have been there all day. She got home from work, and there they were, bold as brass; now the police want witnesses as to how they got in."

Her words came out in a rush of excitement. Gav didn't look remotely excited; his face held an expression of what might be a permanent state of disinterest. Had we said the house were on fire with twenty lap dancers trapped inside needing him to be a hero and rescue them, I doubt the expression would have changed much, if at all.

He leant forward to get a good look at the group clustered at my front door. "Nah, didn't see anything."

6.

Court orders can take weeks to enforce, sometimes even months. It seemed I faced the choice of moving in with Yan and family or residing at a friend's house in the next street. I rang work to explain I would need a few days off to deal with the situation, only to be met with stony indifference from Joseph, my line manager.

"You do realise this is a difficult time; what with Syum being off sick and the thing that happened to Ralph?"

The thing that happened to Ralph, the poor man who hated living so much he ended it, dramatically. Perhaps if any of us took more notice of one another, we might have spotted his unhappiness. Nothing had been learnt. Did Joseph have any idea how I felt right now, having my home invaded by strangers and finding myself homeless?

"I know, I know."

I could imagine his stubby fingers circling the air as he spoke, "We're short-staffed, and we can't afford to be. Any other time, Jayne."

"Well, it's not like you can choose a time for squatters to move in; they just kind of arrive when you least expect it, not that you would expect it, not in a million flaming years."

"Did you lock the house up when you left for work yesterday, Jayne?"

Blame. So now it had become my fault; it was my carelessness that caused the problem. How typical. Despite this, I knew there was every possibility I had left the pantry window open; I had a mental block when it came to that window.

"Whether I did or not, the situation remains the same, Joe. The police said it's been happening quite a bit around this way."

Joseph sniggered, "Ironic considering what we do."

"The irony hadn't passed me by." My tone hurled cold lumps of ice his way.

"Well, if you can manage a few hours here, it would be something, I suppose. Can't you get a neighbour to keep an eye on them?"

He made this sound like I had pets that needed feeding and letting out to pee.

I thought of my sole choice, Gav.

I'd spent the night at my friend Olivia's poky flat a street away from my own. Olivia lived alone, so me staying wasn't a problem. Even though I had to sleep on a broken futon in the sitting room with her massive cat, Humphrey, pressing against my chest, I felt incredibly grateful.

Olivia and I hardly knew one another. We'd met at needlework classes and shared a penchant for wildlife designs. She wore heavy square glasses and punctuated all her sentences with 'y'know'. She worked as a secretary for a large firm of accountants but, luckily for me, happened to be on a week's leave. After speaking to Joseph, I called her and explained his concerns about me having time off.

"Aw no, don't you worry, pet." Her Geordie tones reassured me. "I'll pop around and check if all is well."

"You don't have to go in." I doubted they would let her in anyway.

"Aw no, I won't do that."

What would Yan make of Olivia? I wondered as I brushed my teeth with a borrowed toothbrush.

The police had finally left, advising me to contact a solicitor and obtain an interim possession order. Yan let me in to gather a few clothes. The air of friendly bonhomie he'd adopted for the police disappeared the moment their car pulled off the kerb.

"You din' wanna do that, no." He growled as I shot up the stairs hoping the old man in my bed had gone.

"Actually, Yan," I yelled back down at him, "I should have done that a lot earlier".

I grabbed a nightdress, a skirt, some tights and underwear while the snorer snored on, oblivious.

Hanzi appeared in the bedroom doorway. "You going?"

His round dark eyes reminded me of my brother's Labrador whenever he left the house without him.

"I have to, Hanzi; I can't stay here. Look, your grandpa is in my bed!"

Hanzi nodded. "I like it here." He said simply and left me to my hurried packing.

By the time I staggered round to Olivia's that night, I felt completely exhausted.

To her credit, she welcomed me in with a big hug, sympathetic murmurings, and a hot mug of sweet tea of the kind I'd imagined making for the plane crash victims I'd dreamt of rescuing.

After a barrage of 'aw bless' comments, I retired to the futon, at first grateful for Humphrey's company, but by 3am I'd wanted to launch him out of the window without a parachute.

My initial plan had been to go back to the house early before I went to work, but having gone to bed at 1am, I woke late, so I ended up walking as fast as I could to my office with an aching neck from lying awkwardly.

The first call from Olivia interrupted a team meeting. Joseph shot me a withering look as my mobile bleeped, but I picked it up and defiantly marched out of the room. He'd wanted me to come to work so he'd have to put up with the interruptions.

Olivia sounded calm. "Nought to worry about pet. I popped round like you said; no sign of life at first, but then the curtain moved, and I saw a light on in the kitchen, so they're still there. It was a bit early, so y'know, I expect they're not all up yet."

I thanked her and returned to the meeting.

When Joseph left the building for another meeting, I rang the solicitor my brother had recommended. Paying for her services would cancel out my long-planned summer trip up the Danube with my old school friend Lottie, but getting my home back was all that mattered right now.

At night, my heartbeats rattled like dice in a cup. I tossed and turned on the futon while Humphrey tried to smother me in purry kisses; Hanzi's large brown pleading eyes haunted me—who knew what Bunica's demented behaviour might lead to next? I imagined Yan filling more holdalls with my belongings and stripping the house bare.

Had I not crossed my threshold that night, they would be faceless foes I could fight with the law's slow support. Now they had names, personalities, and stories that made me ponder every action I sought to take.

Small comfort came from the fact that Society would naturally share my self-righteous indignation at this affront to my privacy and ownership rights, and that sense would prevail that an Englishwoman's home is her castle.

Questions strode around in my brain, gesturing hands in the air, twirling and beckoning for me to come up with the answers. What did I really want from life? Why did I do a job I hated? Were my possessions so important to me that I would turf an entire family out on the street? Where would I live if I let them stay?

When daylight finally filtered through Olivia's floral curtains, any chance of sleep had fluttered away.

Realising Olivia would want to sleep late, I flicked on the TV. I kept the sound low and dozed as the breakfast presenters flickered in front of me. Humphrey clawed sleepily at my arm.

Then suddenly, I heard my name mentioned, not by anyone in the room, but by one of the news team on TV.

7

Yan stood on my doorstep, framed by weeds that seemed to have grown a foot in a week. You notice these things when you realise your house is being scrutinised by what might be the entire country, if not the world.

He spoke to the reporter calmly and confidently, as if he were accustomed to being on TV.

Thank goodness it wasn't raining; no one would see how badly the gutter leaked. I hugged my knees to my chest, my mouth wide open, my eyes and brain agog.

"Oh yes," said Yan, his thick, wiry eyebrows meeting like bulls in a field. "We live here; she's the landlady. I no see her since the other night. She wan' us go immediately but no fair, we have a contract."

He waved a sheet of A4 paper. "I got fameeely," he clutched a terrified-looking Hanzi to his side. "My in-law mamma, she no well." He pointed to his temple.

"Oh, that's your place, pet?" Olivia settled herself on the futon beside me. "That was quick; I only phoned late yesterday, y'know."

My mouth gaped even wider. "You called the TV people?"

"I couldn't see it go on, y'know, what with you being so stressed with those people taking over your home. It's just not right. I went around a couple of times during the day, and that Yan chap kept scowling through the window at me. I could only imagine what they were up to in there. I thought a bit of publicity might move things along faster, what with you being in immigration an' all that, it's a good story for the local news channels."

She sat wearing a threadbare nightgown left over from the 1950s, or 'vintage', as she put it, striped pop socks, and some sort of turban. Her glasses perched precariously on the end of her nib-like nose.

"You didn't give them your address?"

"Had to pet; first thing they ask."

Firemen who scramble for a fire alert could not move faster than I did in that moment.

"You might want to get dressed." I yelled. "They'll be here in a minute."

Olivia stared at me, shocked. "You really think so?"

"Yes, I bloody do."

I can't remember getting dressed while sitting in bed since school days, when there wasn't any central heating. It's not so easy when age robs you of teenage suppleness. After a few minutes of strenuous movement, I almost looked respectable, while Olivia looked no different.

"Well, it's not me they'll be wanting; it's you."

Those words plunged me into such a lonely state; I felt tears well. I should ring Joseph, I thought. Then thought again. What would be the point? I'd had a little PR training, but I wasn't sure if it would be sufficient for this situation.

"Who did you call?"

"Oh, just the local press. I don't know how the TV got hold of it all. I'm sorry if I've made more trouble, but I thought it would get them out of there quicker."

I knew that I should go home and face up to this before Yan had the nation on his side, The poor tenant with a mad landlady who apparently tried to evict a family with children and a sick elderly grandmother.

It seemed I had a lot to fight against.

Olivia offered to come with me, but I declined. In the end, I would have to face the consequences. Since my divorce I'd created a rigid outer shell entitled 'coping'.

Bunica hadn't been able to finish her reading.

The last card, the Eight of Swords, probably still lay uninterpreted on the dining table.

I wondered about the card and pondered its meaning. I thought about what it might have meant that we were interrupted seconds before I had received Bunica's reading. Maybe I wasn't meant to know.

The universe intervened. These thoughts churned as I strode through the early mist back to my house.

Not that it felt like my house anymore. I examined my feelings like a fishmonger picking through bones. This whole situation brought with it a strange kind of freedom. I'd been able to step back and think about what I possessed and what it really meant to me. So many questions.

For too long I'd been engrossed in a routine I endured rather than enjoyed.

This intense thought processing made the brief walk even swifter.

I looked up, and there was my house.

By the time I walked up my garden path, camera crews were drawing away in their vans, apparently oblivious to my identity. A small warm feeling of relief restored my confidence.

Not for the first time, I hammered on my own front door. Hanzi and Vadoma appeared at the window. Vadoma's face a scowl in contrast to Hanzi's broad grin. I signalled for him to let me in. He gestured for me to go to the back of the house.

I scanned the kitchen; not a pot or pan littered the work surfaces, everything neat and tidy. Hanzi whispered, "Tată sleep."

I nodded; I could see his fear and wanted to protect him. "It's ok, I let myself in," I winked. "Is Bunica awake?"

Vadoma's voice came from the hallway, "Come here; Bunica wants see you."

The old lady sat at the dining room table in the same chair; I wondered if she had ever left it in all the time I'd been gone. The tarot cards lay neatly in a pile before her. Without meeting my gaze, she gestured with her forefinger for me to sit beside her. Vadoma sat down again, and Hanzi stood at my shoulder. No one had drawn the curtains; the room lay half dark, with shards of silver light from the greyness outside creating beams almost directly onto the cards, or carti as they called them.

Bunica cut the cards into two separate piles and then shuffled them together. She passed me the pack. Vadoma nodded at me. "Now you."

So I shuffled them too. I had never been a card player, but I had watched my father shuffle when playing bridge with his friends, so I had a vague idea of what to do. After I clumsily shuffled the cards, I handed them back to Bunica, who held them for some moments before beginning to spread them out on the table. A heavy silence enveloped us, suggesting that something significant was about to happen. In the split second I thought of the Eight of Swords, the very same card landed face up in front of me. A collective gasp went around the table. Snow White, who'd come to join us without me noticing until now, clasped her hand to her mouth. Hanzi whispered to me, "Carti from before." As if the fact might have been lost on me.

Bunica continued to lay out the cards, her expression never changing as her small mouth formed its usual sucked-in zero shape.

The Hermit, The Ace of Wands, and several other cards, none of which gave me any clue as to their meaning, were patted gently onto the oak. I knew that whatever I might be about to be told, I would welcome it, good or bad; I needed something to tell me to change course in life because I'd never had the courage to do it myself. Here in the company of strangers, perhaps I would discover things about myself I'd chosen to ignore all along.

We all listened intently as Vadoma translated in whispers, and my heartbeat quickened.

8.

I know some people spend their lives following their dreams, while others slavishly follow routine; then there are those that manage a bit of both. Until Yan and family chose my abode as their next place of residence, I had spent my life as a timetable masochist. This could potentially explain the breakdown of my marriages. I refused to be persuaded to leave the security of employment and a home to pursue dreams.

In all honesty, I didn't have any dreams—at least, none that I believed I could realise.

As it turned out, realising I was deadly dull was quite unsettling.

Later that day, I found out the potential reason my work colleague had taken his life.

An old friend of his came to retrieve a few of his personal items from the office. The man smiled in what I took to be an almost forgiving way; his damp-cornered eyes and handsome, frayed-about-the-edges look had a compelling charm.

As he rolled a glass paperweight belonging to the deceased between his palms, he told us about Ralph's drug habit, which, as he described it, turned out to be more of a serious addiction than a habit. Tom, the world-weary man standing forlornly in our midst, described how Ralph, as a young man, had wanted to be an actor, but his all-controlling parents had done everything to thwart his plans.

"All they were interested in", he said, "was that Ralph would one day be like them : own house, investments, a wife and two children, the perfect son to tell their friends about, created in their own image." He paused, seemingly to appraise my reaction to this, as if wondering if I might somehow be insulted. The hairs on the back of my neck prickled; I nodded and forced a smile to encourage him to continue.

"Of course, all of those things are OK, if that's what you want." His deep, lilting voice paused again for a second as if pondering what people here in the room might want.

I glanced over at Joseph just in time to catch him roll his eyes.

"But living a life that didn't allow him to explore something that fed his soul crushed Ralph's spirit; he should have ignored them or even lived out his dreams in his spare time, but having been told not to live in a 'fantasy world' for so long, he eventually escaped in an altogether destructive, rather than constructive, way."

Tom's eyes dropped to the paperweight; at this point I could hardly bear to look at him.

His voice was weak and regretful. "Ralph was a lovely man, not weak but not strong enough to rebel. The power we can wield over one another is truly terrifying. His parents are distraught."

With the minimum of effort, Joseph leant forward and stretched out his hand to shake Tom's. "We're sorry for your loss—well, our loss, too." He muttered. "Ralph was, er, nice to work with."

Joseph's brief handshake appeared dismissive. I sighed inwardly at his gaucheness. He couldn't care less.

My cheeks flushed.

Tom nodded, gathered the paltry collection of Ralph's things and headed to the door.

"I'll see you out." I hurried after him, keen to show that we did care even though we obviously hadn't bothered to find out the first thing about Ralph.

Tom turned to me when we reached the bottom stair, "Do you really like what you do here?"

"Well, I don't mind it; it pays the bills." I didn't want to appear negative. "At the moment I think they're going to be rather high, as squatters have taken over my home, well, gypsies to be exact."

I'm not sure why I felt compelled to share this information with a stranger, but before I knew it, the words had spilt out.

Tom stared as if waiting for me to declare this a joke. I stared back, not blinking.

"Say it again." He eyed me with surprise. "So where are you living? Not with them?"

"No! On a cramped-up futon at my friend Olivia's flat, whose cat Humphrey thinks I am a human hot water bottle gift from his owner."

He shook his head in apparent disbelief. "How bizarre."

As if acting independently of me, my mouth said, "If you buy me a coffee, I'll tell you all about it."

I hoped he wouldn't find this too forward, but he nodded with a smile. "Just say when."

After work, Tom met me at a café we both knew, roughly halfway between my office and Olivia's. I arrived five minutes late, but I took a moment to watch him through the window before I entered; his shoulders were hunched over the table, and his chin rested in one hand. He looked as if he carried the weight of the world on his shoulders.

Unsurprising, really. I fleetingly wondered if he and Ralph had been more than friends but dismissed the idea immediately. The way he looked at me told me something I barely dared hope for.

Tom didn't see me when I entered, and I gently touched his shoulder to make him aware of my presence.

A pristine waitress with her hair in a tight bun skipped over to take our order.

I ordered two coffees and a Danish pastry for myself. Tom wasn't hungry.

"Ralph's death must have been such a shock?"

"Not really; you could tell he had given up."

I hadn't realised anything about Ralph except that he drank nettle tea; annoyingly, he used to leave the bag on the draining board in the office kitchen, and he gazed out of the window a lot during meetings, but didn't we all?

Tom's gaze locked mine, his eyes a hazy blue. "What about you, though? You seem to be in quite a spot."

I gave a humourless laugh. "You could say that—after what happened this morning, I'm certainly in no hurry to go back there." I paused, wondering what he would make of it all and if I'd done the right thing by inviting him to hear about my bizarre situation. The poor man had enough to contend with already.

My expression obviously concerned him. "What happened?"

"I'm surprised you didn't see it on the television news." Even a few of the papers had picked up the story. I'd had a string of messages on my voicemail asking for an interview. I'd ignored them; Joseph had told me to.

Tom's eyes narrowed with concern. "You look pale."

When I told him about Bunica squatting in the dining room, a sudden wave of disloyalty washed over me.

9

The Eight of Swords flipped upwards first. The picture on the card shows a woman blindfolded and bound, surrounded by eight swords pushed into the ground. Bunica shook her head slightly when she saw this card again; she muttered at Vadoma, but Vadoma's thin lips tightened.

I knew I must be patient.

Bunica spun the card to face me. Snow White leant forward, and I could feel Hanzi's breath on my neck. With a palm to her cheek, Bunica burbled at Vadoma for a few moments, then lifted swimmy pupils in my direction, but it seemed obvious she wasn't focusing on me at all.

Hanzi whispered in my ear, "She's speaking with spirits."

Then Vadoma began, "You, in your thinks."

"Thoughts." I corrected.

"Yuh, thoughts— you bind up with no helpful thoughts. But you have choices. See the path in front woman is clear. You think you got no strength, no power, but you do. You put yourself here, like this." She gestured with her hands to form a corner. "But you no have to stay like that, no!" Her words came out forcefully in her determination to make me understand.

Bunica rattled off some more in her deep, guttural garblings.

"You are a strong woman; you can do what you want, but you no see that. You must think; you are not how you say, *a victim,* but you can do more what you want."

I smiled. We are all bound by our thoughts, but what we think we need is perhaps not what we actually need. It can be all too easy to sleepwalk through life. Funny that I'd been thinking this way lately, and now I had confirmation.

Bunica pushed the Eight of Swords aside. The Hermit card was next, which I found very apt; she hardly needed to explain it to me. Seclusion (not that Vadoma knew that word), isolation, or "just you, no person else", as she more simply put it, was exactly what I expected.

Bunica's shrivelled mouth stretched into a grin, and her arm reached out, sweeping a card under my nose; it showed a hand reaching out of a cloud to grasp a stick; the stick had leaves and twigs growing out of it. For some reason, Bunica appeared quite delighted with this card, chuckling away and tapping the table with excitement.

Vadoma's mealy-mouthed expression didn't change, but she raised an eyebrow. "She likes this card: happy carti, Ace of Wands."

I nodded, as I could only imagine it carried positive messages.

"Now is the time – *you* choose; *you* do something." Vadoma struggled with the words, her lack of language as frustrating for her as it was for me. "You do what you wan'; you get what you wan'." She nodded furiously at me. "Is very good Carti; you mus' do well."

I made a mental note to buy a book on the meanings of these cards. I'd never paid much attention to psychics, the Tarot or any such nonsense, as I had previously thought it to be. The revelation of these cards at this precise moment struck me as a remarkable coincidence. I laughed to myself that perhaps the next card would show a group of people leaving a house and show how the guttering had been fixed and the weeds pulled out.

"Oh, you no laugh! This what the spirits say for you is important – listen!"

Suddenly, Bunica thumped the table with a heavy thwack, impressively forceful for such a frail lady; her head rolled back, her eyes shut, and a tiny pink tongue formed an arrow shape under her top lip.

A noise came from her like no other sound I'd ever heard. A deep throttled back of the throat splutter, as if she were trying to rid herself of some terrible demon deep inside. Her head rolled forward onto her chest, and she grasped at the pendant beneath her chin. In a single movement, she tore it from her neck, causing the leather strap to snap. Her hand hit the table and pushed the pendant in my direction. As it came closer, I saw that it appeared to be a small leather pouch. Vadoma gasped and pressed a fist to her mouth. Hanzi stood rigid behind me, and Snow White recoiled from the table. We all watched in horror as the ancient Bunica's cloth-covered head slumped down before us, her face turned towards me, her eyes wide open and filmy.

I tentatively reached out for her wrist. I had completed a short first aid course many years ago, so I knew I should check for a pulse. I couldn't find one. I pushed myself up off the chair, my legs weak and my hands shaking. No one else moved or uttered a word.

I felt her neck but again couldn't feel a pulse.

"Hanzi, pass me my bag."

"What you do?" Vadoma remained transfixed in her seat, her back straight, her eyes round.

"I'm calling emergency services; I think she might be…" I couldn't bring myself to say the word dead.

I dialled 999, and as I did so, I noticed the time. So absorbed was I in my early morning tarot reading I had completely forgotten I had a meeting to attend at ten o'clock, with only twenty minutes left to get there.

"Oh no, I've got to go; I'm late!"

Snow White leant forward to kiss her grandmother's head; Hanzi stood by her, tears spilling down his cheeks.

Vadoma remained seated, seemingly frozen in stone.

As I reached the front door, I remembered Yan. I shouted up the stairs to him, urging him to come down. I remembered the old man who had taken to my bed. The thought crossed my mind that Yan might be upstairs attending to a similar situation. For a brief moment, I considered running up the stairs to see what was going on, but Joseph's likely annoyance at my tardiness overcame me, and after making another pleading call up the stairs to Yan, I swiftly left through the front door.

It's amazing how shock can make us act. I started to run; reaching the end of the street, I tried to wave down a taxi on the main road, but the traffic was hardly moving. As I searched frantically for a black cab, I saw an ambulance trying to make its way through the traffic, blue lights flashing, the driver's mouth moving in curses as a middle-aged man in a Jaguar blocked the way. The man, chatting away on his mobile phone, seemed oblivious to the emergency vehicle's plight even though he must have heard the sirens. I trotted over to the stationary car and tapped furiously on the passenger window. The man looked up at me, his mouth half open, saying something into his phone. I gesticulated wildly. He flung the mobile on to the seat beside him and pulled over to let the ambulance past.

I stood still a moment to watch the ambulance turn into my street, and it occurred to me that it wasn't an emergency anyway. Bunica lay dead on my dining room table. Somehow her death seemed less shocking than when she defecated in the corner of the room. Even now, I can see the annoyance on the Jaguar driver's face, his pink tie, and his immaculate white cuffs. As I clambered gratefully into a taxi, I couldn't help but wonder what that same man would have made of my morning so far.

I reached the office eighteen minutes late. Joseph had started the meeting, and a number of irritable murmuring people sat waiting for me. They looked like an unwilling jury summoned to hear a tedious case. For the first time in my work history, I could have entertained them with my fantastical tales of the past few days by way of explanation. Until now, I'd never needed an explanation for tardiness, as my life generally functioned seamlessly. As tempting as it was, Joseph's set jaw forbade any such indulgence.

I hardly heard a word spoken throughout the hour of a monotonously droning man, intermittently scrawling hieroglyphics on a whiteboard. The notes on my pad made little sense, and when asked for input, I rambled on about statistics that everyone had likely heard many times before.

Then when I'd arrived back in my office, Tom was there to collect Ralph's things.

10

Tom walked me back home. The pavements were a little slippery as darkness had robbed any remaining warmth from the air. He clutched my elbow a couple of times to steady me as my smooth-soled shoes skidded.

"They really are useless in this weather." My nervous gabble created silvery little puffs in the air.

It wasn't easy recounting Bunica's sudden death, especially when Tom had so recently lost Ralph. I had to tell him, of course; I couldn't just pretend it hadn't happened, and he'd been so intent on the whole tarot experience that I had no way of winding off the story in any fictitious way.

We walked in intermittent silence, me reflecting on Bunica's readings and what we might find when we arrived outside of my house, with occasional prompts from Tom whenever I began to stutter.

The dark circles beneath his eyes told me all I needed to know about how he was coping with the loss of his friend.

I felt incredibly grateful that he had insisted on accompanying me back to the house. For the first time in a long time, I was glad to have a man taking charge, and for a change, it was in the right sort of way.

I remembered I should phone Olivia to say I'd be late. She would no doubt be worrying but not wanting to disturb me with a call. I put my hand on Tom's arm to stop him from speaking while I called her to prevent a deluge of questions about who I was with.

I kept it brief.

"Yes, I'm not sure what time I'll be back. Yes, I'll let you know when I'm on my way."

Finally we reached my house. I could see candles flicker in the gap in the curtains. I guided Tom to the back of the house, where we found Hanzi, Yan and the old man from my bed gathered around a small bonfire. None of them looked up as we approached. We entered the house through the kitchen door; the air felt cold. Vadoma and Snow White sat hands clasped, eyes shut at the dining room table, surrounded by candles. I couldn't help but wonder where they'd found all the matches. The local newsagent rarely stocked more than a box or two.

I looked around, half expecting to find Bunica laid out in a coffin, but there was no sign of her. I put a hand on Vadoma's shoulder. "I'm so sorry." I should have said this ten hours earlier.

She nodded, her eyes still closed.

Tom shuffled his feet behind me.
"I brought a friend with me. I er didn't know what to do. I'm sorry I had to go off to work, but there was an important meeting." What a stupid thing to say, I thought. "Have you eaten?"
Snow White sorrowfully shook her head.

"I could get us a takeaway?" Tom suggested helpfully.

Both of them mournfully shook their heads in response. I felt that we should leave them to it and turned to Tom to signal our exit. As I gathered my bag, Vadoma flung her arm out to me and clutched at my hand. I thought she wanted to hold it for comfort, but instead, she thrust a small object into my palm and forcibly closed my fingers. "Putsi, Bunica wants you have it; it is her luck charm."

I felt a small leather pouch graze against my skin and wondered what it held inside.

My typical British inbred politeness forced me to object, "Oh no," I said, and "I couldn't possibly." However, Vadoma's determined glare forced me to accept. "Thank you." I muttered softly.

I turned to leave, but then Vadoma spat out a single word at me. "Tea."

"Tea? Of course, I'll make some."
"Then you leave."

I made tea for all of them. Tom and I took the tea to the men gathered at the bonfire, who silently accepted it. They paid no attention to the stranger in their midst. This sounds like a strange phrase to repeat, but they had made my home their own, so whoever I brought to them could only be described as a stranger.

We left the house and walked to Olivia's. An animated Tom bombarded me with questions.

"What are you going to do about them? How long do you think they'll stay? Is there a court order?"

I could only answer the third question.

I felt the putsi in my pocket. I turned it over in my fingers, wondering what it might contain.

"And where did they take the body?"

"I can only assume the mortuary." I didn't have the courage to ask in case they'd laid her out to rest on my bed.

I had forgotten to ring Olivia. Oh well, we were there now.

If she hadn't taken to changing into her dressing gown every time she entered the flat, she might not have been so alarmed to see Tom by my side. I had forgotten the weird and not-so-wonderful attire she liked to wear. The traumas and revelations of the day clouded my mind. She hid behind the bedroom door, her face smothered in the mud she used as a face pack, only occasionally peeking out.

I introduced Tom.

Now we were in sight of the futon, and I badly wanted to lie on it; my temples ached, and I wanted to be alone. Tom sat clutching the glass of wine I'd poured for him, staring at the floor. I guessed he was probably wondering how he'd come to end up here. What a day for him. What a day for me!

"I'll drink this, and then I'd better go."

I nodded, not quite knowing what to say.

"If you need any help, I know a competent lawyer."

I muttered my thanks.

The next day I woke up early. I hadn't set my alarm, and now I realised this was because it was Saturday. I pushed Humphrey off my pillow, pulled the garish floral dressing gown Olivia had lent me around my shoulders, and shuffled into the kitchen to make tea. The day between the blinds hadn't quite woken either; a cold blue light showed above the rooftops. Olivia had one of those retro kettles in pink; I placed it on her little gas stove and waited for the whistle. Humphrey pushed around my legs, so I filled a saucer with food pellets and passed them down to him.

Tea, toast and a scan of the papers passed the first hour of the day. I explained to Olivia about Bunica and why Tom had trailed in my wake the night before; then, arm in arm, we slowly walked back to my house. We waited until 11 o'clock, figuring it would take time for them to rouse themselves, especially if they'd been up half the night in mourning.

The street seemed quite lively; a couple of children took turns on a bike, and a furniture truck was parked up on a kerb with two men huffing and heaving a sofa along the pavement. I spotted Gav cleaning a car, not his own, but something far flashier.

Despite the churning depths of its interior over the past few days, the house still looked familiar. We entered through the back door, as I had taken to doing so since the new occupiers had arrived.

Silence met us, a heavy emptiness as if all souls had fled. My heart missed a beat. I called out for Vadoma; no answer. I moved through the hall shouting for Yan; no answer. No Hanzi stood with his sad brown eyes, no Snow White clutching a plate, no Boldo lolling on the rug. I told Olivia to check around the ground floor while I ran upstairs, still expecting to find the old man askance in my bed. He'd gone. I even checked the bathroom; no one remained.

Downstairs, Olivia sat at the dining room table, examining three cards: The Ace of Wands, The Hermit, and the Eight of Swords.

I fell into the nearest chair and wept, though whether it was with relief or loss, I cannot tell you.

The Putsi

1.

Eighteen years, three months, and two days is the exact period of time that passed before Hanzi suddenly and unexpectedly appeared in my life again.

My thirtieth exhibition, a cause for celebration, meant that a multitude of friends had turned up to enjoy a glass of champagne and carefully chosen nibbles. Tom painstakingly sought an exceptional gallery in west London to mark the occasion, and he found an incredible venue. He knew the gallery would instantly captivate me. He'd installed stained glass windows designed and created by a local craftsman. He had personally applied whitewash to all the walls. He'd chosen LED spotlights that beamed light as clear as day onto my works, showing them to their full advantage.

Fabulous art glass stood on pillars—sculptures in colours he knew I adored. It had been a labour of true, determined love—love I had been totally immersed in for the past eighteen years.

Of course I'd known Tom's late hours and busy weekends were taken up with his plan to make this particularly notable exhibition the most special to date. Tom had made all of them uniquely memorable, and every time I swooned in awe of his imagination and passion to 'get things right', as he put it. As each exhibition closed, I would wonder to myself what he would come up with next. Every time he made me greedy to see what scene he would invent to show off my works.

This time, as well as the stunning windows and art glass, he'd arranged for choristers, all in white, to serenade the opening, with the theme of this exhibition being religious artefacts and spiritual emblems. Their voices were so pure and resonant that a moment came when I thought one of the art glass sculptures might leap off a pillar and shatter on the beautifully stained floorboards beneath.

For some years now, as my mortal coil shortened and the lines on my face etched corridors of all the emotions I'd ever experienced, some less deep than others, my fascination with the afterlife had translated through to my art. I'd experimented with needlework, oils, and printmaking to express the fear, the loathing of my former existence, and the later-life calm I'd come to enjoy. Now my focus had transferred to what might come next. The objects we choose for solace and the visions of a parallel existence that also occupy our thoughts. As you might expect, images from the tarot also featured.

I'd never gone to another Tarot reader after my experience with Bunica. Somehow it didn't seem the right thing to do. Instead, I studied the cards myself, but with a more artistic eye rather than a need to find out more about destiny. The main thing I'd taken from my experience with the Romanian gypsy family who briefly and without invitation had occupied my home all those years ago was to examine my life in extreme detail. The conclusion of my self-examination had been illuminating and powerful enough to make me change course, just as the Eight of Swords had suggested.

Chewing on a salmon and caviar-topped blini, I surveyed the room of people who eighteen years ago I did not know. The room heaved with a menagerie of artistic types, dealers, collectors, local business folk, a couple of photographers, and a girl from one of the national papers, who constantly whispered into her smartphone. She, in particular, made me nervous. Her tight little mouth and close-set eyes appeared to approve of nothing they surveyed. I saw her wince when eating a chilli-infused spring roll, shrug at a piece I felt particularly proud of and sneer at one of the art glass vases. Evidently, she was unaware of the existence of Eva Zeisel, a Hungarian artist who is considered a genius by me and many others. If you could produce stunning designs when you reach one hundred years old, then perhaps I will give you a licence to sneer, I mumbled into my champagne flute. Come to think of it, I doubted she could produce anything of note at this young age, other than critical words in an attempt to appear clever or cool. Perhaps I might be unkind; I reviewed assumptions. After all, I might find her praising my work in tomorrow's press. But no, even if she did, I still wouldn't like her, purely for her manners this evening.

"What are you frowning at?" Tom appeared at my side. His handsome face had barely changed over the years.

"Oh, nothing." I muttered, dropping my gaze from the girl.

"Don't let the art critic worry you. You should know by now that the art world loves what you do, and so do the people who happily and regularly buy your pieces. Newsprint holds no value. The pigeons will be picking out the fattest chips they can find from it in no time at all."

I laughed. Tom always managed to treat any fear or suspicion I had with throwaway humour designed to comfort me.

"It's the comments online I worry about. They're in the ether forever."

"It's pathetic, isn't it? How insecure I feel, even after all this time."

"There is not a pathetic thing about you." He dropped a kiss on my head and steered me towards friends he knew would stroke the artistic ego that I had steadily grown with each exhibition.

Olivia reached out her hand for mine. "If I buy this picture over here, can I pay you in installments?" She led me over to a long horizontal embroidered piece depicting angels and warriors fighting in unison against a dragon called Envy. "You know, of course, I might die before the final instalment, but I'll make sure the balance gets paid off via my will."

I laughed. Dear Olivia had grown ever more eccentric over the years. At least she hadn't turned up in one of her famous dressing gowns holding her latest beloved cat. Humphrey had long since passed to a better life, but now Olivia had "re-homed" an overweight ginger tom she'd named Aubrey. When I say re-home, I mean stolen from a neglectful neighbour.

"For goodness sake, Liv, have it! I don't need the money." I whispered in her ear. This wasn't entirely true, but I knew she struggled to afford basics at times, let alone expensive artworks. This hadn't stopped her scrimping to help me out by buying pieces in my early days, determined to see me a success.

She grinned dementedly. "For real? I insist on paying you *something*."

"You've bought loads from me and been such a wonderful friend. I *insist*. Have it as an anniversary present."

We hugged.

What would I have done without Olivia when I'd had to run from my house as a fugitive in the night?

As I turned away from her, I spotted a blue-suited man with his nose pressed up against a painting I'd created only a few weeks before. Roughly cut dark curls spilt over the collar of his white shirt. He turned his head a moment, and I noticed a slight dent in the bridge of his nose. I couldn't take my eyes off him; he seemed familiar, and yet I couldn't place him. I stood entranced, racking my brain for clues. I frequently caught myself forgetting names, which I found to be an annoying and embarrassing habit.

Seemingly aware of being watched, he pivoted to face me.

The moment became cinematic. Everyone in the room carried on talking, but their chatter fell silent to the heroine's ears, a freeze frame, as her expression froze with sudden recognition. Scene-stopping drama: all actors were directed to stop their conversations and halt action so the most dramatic part of the story could unfold.

"Hanzi!"

2.

Seeing a man you last encountered as a boy without any in-between meetings to adjust to his maturity is a strange experience. My lasting memories of Hanzi were his Labrador eyes and nervous grin.

I could still hear him say, "But we like it here, lady." I remembered his slight frame and dark curls. The curls remained, but he was no longer slight. His shoulders were as wide as his father's now, his body muscular beneath the suit; the length of his legs propelled him to a height a full head higher than my own.

How do you greet someone who wasn't a friend, who, in a way, once was a kind of enemy?

I never viewed Hanzi as an enemy, just a boy caught up in a family that did what it wanted, regardless of the law.

I reached out a hand, and Hanzi firmly grasped it.

Despite all that had passed before, I felt jubilant to see him again. I had wondered many times over the years what his fate might have been. Never for one moment did I imagine he might have thought about me.

Flashbacks took me to the moment the Eight of Swords overturned on my dining room table, his breath on my neck, and his awe at the card's repeat appearance.

But was he here by accident or design?

Maybe this was a happy coincidence.

"Hanzi, are you a fan of art?"

Or in other words, *what are you doing here?*

"I very much like your art."

His mouth stretched into a broad grin, and immediately I saw his father, Yan, on my doorstep, charming the police.

A nugget of discomfort rolled in my belly.

I looked around for Tom, but he had disappeared. Olivia was engrossed in conversation with two elderly ladies.

"Ah, thank you. That's, um, great."

"Yes, I am here because I saw a little of you on TV. I wanted to see for myself your art." He laughed a little. "And you? How are you?"

"I often wondered about you, Hanzi, and your family. You all left so suddenly." I searched for more words to explain how I felt when I found them all gone. I couldn't work out how to express all that had happened in the aftermath of their disappearance in just a few sentences.

"So you saw the piece about the exhibition and thought you'd come along?"

"The piece?"

"On TV."

"Oh yes, that is right. It was a surprise to see you after all this time, but you look so much the same." He smiled again, and it seemed more genuine this time. I realised he must feel as awkward as I did, if not more so.

I laughed nervously. It felt very odd talking to Hanzi as a man.

"I've got so many questions to ask, but now really isn't the time or place." I smiled, apologetically. I gestured to the people around us as if I needed a magic wand to make them disappear.

Hanzi nodded. He'd been standing in what a sergeant major might call an 'at ease' position with his hands clasped behind his back, upright, legs a little apart. The smart suit and white shirt made me wonder what he did now, but as I'd just commented, this moment wasn't the best time to find out all I wanted to know.

"There's a coffee shop on the corner of this street; I think it's called 'Millies'. Could we meet there at 11 o'clock tomorrow morning to catch up?"

Hanzi's face screwed up with apparent confusion. "You want to meet me in a *café*?"

I nodded, wondering why this should be such a strange request.

"I want to come to your house. I want to see the things I saw when I was a boy— the goblets, the cricket bat, things like that." His eyes darkened with disappointment as if he had reckoned on the situation being a given when he found me again. He'd envisioned walking into the same house, no doubt, to find everything as he remembered.

I laughed apologetically. "Oh Hanzi, I don't live in the same house, but yes, I do still have those things you saw."

I'd found Yan's holdall full of my things still in the house after they'd all disappeared.

The potential risk of letting him into my current home spun in my head. It hadn't been Hanzi who had decided to break into my house, change the locks, and illegally occupy my residence. However, the thought of inviting him to my new home left me feeling uneasy. I thought it over quickly; I couldn't imagine him turning up with his whole family and expecting to dwell there. While his smile reminded me of his father's, nothing else did. His attire, apparent charm, and articulation were significantly different from those of his father.

When Hanzi's family vanished as suddenly as they had arrived, I chose not to move back in to my house. The thought of living there again made me feel odd; I'd been displaced and couldn't return. I immediately put it on the market and rented a flat in the same block of flats where Olivia lived. The house sold quickly despite the negative publicity. The street had been in a desirable part of the city, and I hadn't been greedy with the asking price.

Too many images flooded to mind when I tried to go back into the house, and I knew I would never be able to live there again. In a way,

Hanzi's family had done me a favour; my life in that house had been merely existence.

In truth, I would probably have lived there to the end of my days if Hanzi's family hadn't taken over. The days stretched out in a repetitive routine, filled with memories of my ill-conceived marriage, a dull, unrewarding job, a life that was safe but boring, and a life that was untrue to myself. If only they had arrived ten years earlier, I thought, then I would have had ten more years of real living. But regrets are pointless; I should be grateful, more than grateful, for every moment of my life since then. I almost felt I owed it to Hanzi to let him in to see my new life.

A few months later I'd bought a picturesque cottage in a village south of the city, and everything changed for the better. Just as the cards foretold.

Like a magician whisking a rabbit out of a hat, I hastily pulled a card out of my purse and passed it to him. "This is my address." I quickly calculated when Tom would be out. "Come on Wednesday evening, then we can talk."

Hanzi nodded; his expression serious. He stared at me a moment, then, without a word, walked steadily out of the exhibition without looking back.

I gazed after him as if in a dream.

Olivia roused me from my reverie. "Who was that?"

" He's a collector. I've not met him before. Nice chap."

Guilt prickled my skin, but I knew Olivia would not approve if I told her the truth, nor would Tom. It felt terrible to lie to the people I loved most, but they would never understand my need to find out what happened to Hanzi and his family once they left my home.

Tom would view it as risky and unnecessary, and Olivia would likely rush to the news-desk at the local paper.

After Hanzi's sudden appearance and our exchange, I found it almost impossible to focus on the exhibition. Talking to people felt like wading through mud. All I could think about was what Hanzi would tell me. What about Vadoma, Yan and Snow White? What had become of them? What did Hanzi do now? Did Hanzi form a new generation that squatted in the homes of strangers and took whatever they saw fit? Looking at him, I didn't think so. He had the look of a businessman, albeit a tousled, slightly wild one. I warned myself not to fall for his attire; he might have worn the suit simply to impress me.

As much as I wanted to connect with him again, I knew I should be on my guard.

My heart quickened at the prospect of Hanzi visiting my new home.

My life had completely transformed; I dressed in a far more flamboyant style than my previous grey-suited office attire. My hair was now carefully coiffed in a slightly undone bun. I even wore eyeliner and rouged my lips. But in a single moment, the boy who had become a man in a world invisible to me had pulled me back eighteen years, and suddenly I was experiencing the sights, sounds, and feelings of the day—I couldn't turn the key in the lock of my front door.

Tom touched my arm, and a frisson of shock passed through me as his presence transported me back to now.

"Everything alright?"

"Yes, fine." I attempted a reassuring smile.

3.

I spent the whole of Wednesday fretting that Tom would change his mind about going to see an old friend for an evening out in Kensington. He'd planned to stay over at his club so they could have a few beers. He hadn't seen this friend in over ten years and didn't seem entirely sure that he wanted to.

"It'll do you good to get away from me for an evening." I tried not to sound too desperate for him to go.

He shot me a wounded look. "You're bored of me then?"

I knew he spoke in jest, but I felt so nervous about Hanzi coming round I snapped back at him. "Just got things to do."

"What things?"

I sighed. Normally, Tom wouldn't subject me to such interrogation, but perhaps he could sense my edginess.

"Nothing really, just a face pack and a book I've been wanting to start for ages." I grinned.

I knew something so dull would send him running for the hills – or at least to his friend.

"I'm feeling a bit worn out—what with the exhibition and all that—and I've got to spend the day ringing people and organising collections and deliveries. As much as I enjoy selling the work, I don't enjoy the administration that goes with it. A night to myself will do me good."

Tom finished his tea and scooped out the last bit of yolk remaining in the boiled egg that constituted his breakfast.

"I can help."

"What, with the face pack and book?"

"No, Silly, with the admin stuff."

"Tom, you do enough already. I'll be fine; I just need to get on with it, and then I can relax this evening — in peace." I added a little weight to the last word to ensure he got the message.

When people say they haven't uttered a cross word in umpteen years of a relationship, I always think there must be something wrong with them. Tom and I experienced our fair share of sharp exchanges, slammed doors, and had the odd day of sulking. We were both adept at sulking, and occasionally it became competitive, with neither of us willing to make up. Our record sulking bout lasted thirty-eight hours and twenty-two minutes, which would likely not even be noteworthy in the Guinness Book of Records. To end the sulking match, one of us would usually do something to make the other laugh.

I hadn't heard from Tom for several weeks when he'd left Olivia's flat and assumed he had no desire to get involved with a woman who'd laden him with her problems at a time he was mourning his friend. The intention hadn't been to get involved with him, even though I did find him attractive. He'd merely been a friendly and kind face at a time when I needed it most. In truth I virtually forgot about him.

Then, unexpectedly, he called me and suggested he buy me dinner.

Without Tom to encourage me in my art and financially support me during the transitional period when I left my job to pursue it, I doubt I could ever have been as successful as I ended up.

The seed of change had been planted with the Eight of Swords tarot card, and and encouraging man to water and nourish its growth came as an added bonus.

Olivia too had shouted from the sidelines, "Go on, girl, you can do it!"

For which, I am eternally grateful.

Every time I wavered or complained my art wasn't good enough to attract the sums I needed to live on, Tom pointed out all the positives and spurred me on to eventual success. I became his project. He felt he'd failed Ralph as his friend by not nagging him enough to pursue his acting dream, so I became his new project and eventually his lover.

Our relationship burnt slowly, but the flame rose higher by the day.

I couldn't remember the last time I'd lied to Tom, apart from the odd white lie about how much I'd spent on an outfit or how many drinks I'd had with Olivia in the pub when I came home a bit drunk in the mid-afternoon. They were just silly little lies.

As the hours ticked by, I cursed myself for lying about Hanzi's visit. If Tom's friend cancelled, what would I do then? I had no contact number for Hanzi and no way of explaining his appearance without admitting I'd lied. How would Tom react to such a deceit— and, in truth, a painfully stupid deceit? And who knew Hanzi's real purpose in tracking me down and insisting on seeing me at my new home?

I felt nauseous, but also excited.

Tom glanced up at me over the top of his laptop. "You alright?"

I forced a reassuring smile. "Yes, of course. Are you?"

He didn't smile back. "You don't seem your usual self."

He didn't identify exactly how he'd reached this conclusion.

"Honestly, I'm fine."

There was nothing honest about me, and I didn't feel remotely fine.

"I'm going to pop over to the studio to wrap some pieces."

I hoped he wouldn't offer to come and help. Luckily he dropped his eyes back to the laptop screen and muttered something about remembering my cardigan. Occasionally he could be a bit too parental.

My studio was in a partially converted barn. A mixture of commissions and good high-value sales over the past couple of years had finally produced enough cash to pay for one half to be transformed into a light and airy space for my 'mess', as I called it.

I liked living out of the city. I never had before, and I regretted the years staring at bricks as I walked to work every day, to my horrible job where all I seemed to do was listen to people argue about their rights and hear miserable stories about where they had come from and were likely to head back to when they didn't have the proper paperwork or visas.

I did not miss working in immigration in any way, shape, or form. Now I could look out for owls, own a cat, and enjoy the sight of wild spring flowers encompassing the cottage as the days grew a little warmer. Out in the fresh air, I didn't feel quite so stifled by my lie. I decided to go for a little walk instead of going straight to the barn. I ambled down the lane thinking I'd visit the local shop to buy Tom some of the ham he liked for lunch.

Immersed in my thoughts, I barely noticed Jed, the farmer, breeze by in his jeep.

I acknowledged Doreen, the local champion chutney maker, and Lucy, a banker's wife, striding past, her long legs accentuated by skinny jeans tucked into pristine green wellies; thereafter, I didn't pass another soul.

The village shop had become a bit of a community effort as the elderly couple who had run it for years became ever more feeble. Today, Aggy, a burly middle-aged woman, was "manning the till," as she put it, and feeding tidbits to her shiny dachshund, Flash. Her customer service skills weren't exactly of a professional calibre; in fact, she bordered on obnoxious, but I suppose you get what you don't pay for with some volunteers.

I grabbed the ham, ferreted some change out of my pocket and put it on the counter, then turned to go, wanting to get out of the shop as quickly as possible.

"There's been a stranger round here asking about where you live." She uttered the words in the true style of all the best thriller films: low, guttural, and in a mildly threatening tone.

"Oh?"

I didn't want to turn the exchange into a conversation but could hardly ignore the comment.

"I am expecting someone, so maybe it was him."

Divulging such information was a terrible idea in a close-knit community, but the words were out before I had time to think them through properly. Maybe it would be better if people knew a stranger had been calling my house. At least if anything untoward happened, someone would have a description and approximate timing.

I hurried out of the shop, back up the lane to the safety of my barn.

4.

Hanzi arrived clutching a bunch of daffodils. He entered tentatively, looking around as if a little lost, or perhaps checking we were really alone.

"I live here with Tom; he came to the house with me the night before you all left. Do you remember?"

Hanzi shook his head. It was a strange night. I remember the fire and everyone being so quiet."

"It must have felt very strange to you as a young boy. I guess you hadn't experienced the loss of a loved one before?"

"An uncle or two; Bunica was different."

"You witnessed her death— a terrible thing for an adult, never mind a young boy."

"In my culture we are expected to act as men, even when we are boys."

"Tea, coffee, beer, wine? What can I get you?" I kept my voice light and confident. This time I would be the one in control.

However, dressed in a black shirt, smart black jeans, and shiny workman-style boots, it was Hanzi who exuded power. A heavy gold amulet hung around his neck; I recognised it as his father's.

"How are your parents?"

He ignored the question. "Is Tom here?"

I had been hoping he wouldn't ask.

"No, he's out for the evening, but he won't be back late." My voice rose an octave with the lie.

Hanzi opted for tea. As I busied myself finding mugs and biscuits, I wondered what he made of my ageing physique. I could feel him studying my every move. When last he'd seen me, I'd been eighteen years younger, but to a young boy's eyes I must have seemed old even then.

"You married Tom?" Hanzi smiled as if marriage would be a good thing.

"No, we never got around to it."

Tom had never asked. Given my unsuccessful first marriage, I avoided the subject.

As far as I knew, Tom had never married.

Hanzi's brow furrowed, but he said nothing. I knew that with his people, "living in sin" wasn't acceptable.

 "What about you, Hanzi? Are you married?"

Hanzi smiled again. "Oh yes, I have two boys."

"What is your wife like?"

Hanzi's smile vanished. "My mother, Vadoma, chose my wife; she is my third cousin."

Given his grave expression, I chose not to press him for any further description.

"How old are your boys?"

"Five and eight years." He fiddled with his cup, ignoring the biscuits I'd placed in front of him. "I want to talk about what happened that day, the day Bunica died."

I sat down facing him. "Go on."

"This is not easy to say. I haven't told anyone at all about what happened, not *ever*. You understand?"

I nodded.

He took a deep breath and continued. "Vadoma, she poisoned Bunica." He waited a moment to see what effect these words would have on me, but I remained silent, so he continued. "She used leaves from the yew tree, and blended them in her tea over a couple of days. Because Bunica was so old and frail, it was not difficult to kill her this way. Vadoma made me find the leaves; I went to a couple of churchyards before I found them."

Vadoma murdered Bunica — what a shock!

Hanzi continued. "Vadoma gave you the putsi."

“Yes, she did.” My voice trembled a little.

“Do you still have it?”

“I think so.”

I had hidden it away in a drawer. I had never been a believer in luck per se, but I kept the putsi close, as the moment and manner in which it was given served as a reminder to count my blessings and cherish every day on this earth.

“Did you ever look in it?”

I searched my memory. For a while I’d kept the putsi in my coat pocket, taking it with me wherever I went. Eventually, of course, I changed coats, and the putsi was transferred to a drawer by my bed.

“Yes, I did look inside. I didn't open it when Vadoma first gave it to me, but I did a few years later. I felt uncomfortable opening someone else’s private purse. It gave me a strange feeling.”

Perhaps this was the real reason Hanzi had come—to reclaim the putsi. The pouch held sentimental value to me, but also it carried a sense of luck I’d never trusted in before.

Since it had been in my possession, everything had gone right for a change: my love life, my career, and my fortunes. But in real terms, it belonged to Hanzi and his family. It was an heirloom he had probably longed to retrieve all these years.

“I suppose you want it back?”

Hanzi smiled. “I don’t like to take it from you.” He looked around, admiring my large kitchen, the range cooker, and the beautiful stone tiles. “It brought the luck Bunica predicted for you.”

“But I am guessing you need that luck now?”

Hanzi's gaze held mine, then he gently shook his head.

5.

The next morning, bright sunlight peeled open my eyelids; a persistent beam through a gap in the curtains rested on my face, and not for the first time, I thought what a wonderful way to wake up.

I stretched out to prod Tom's arm but remembered he wasn't there to make the tea this morning.

A bird chirped merrily in the sycamore tree by the bedroom window - spring at last. After an icy winter, treacherous roads and stockpiling at the supermarket, better weather brought a real sense of relief. As soon as my eyes opened, that was it for me; I had to be up. Gone were the days when I'd reset the snooze button umpteen times to cadge extra minutes of sleep. These days, I could look forward to the beautiful surrounding countryside, my artwork, and Tom ambling around the place working on his latest project, whatever it might be.

I mulled over the night before and all that Hanzi had told me. In our world we would call the police and start a murder investigation, but Hanzi said that Vadoma had long since died of alcohol poisoning. The guilt of her evil deed became too much for her, and she lost herself in drink. Yan had also passed away. Ever bullish, he'd picked on the wrong man in a street fight, unsurprisingly over property. The man beat him to death.

Such brutal stories, I felt terrible for Hanzi.

Snow White continued to produce children. As far as Hanzi knew, she had given birth to six children. He didn't see her all that often; she travelled with her husband's family now. I'd listened with fascination as Hanzi told me many stories of what they'd endured, sleeping rough, finding food wherever they could, fights, and court orders (not that they ever went to court.) Boldo the dog had somehow stayed with them and managed to die of old age, a better fate than Yan and Vadoma, at least.

I promised to find the putsi for Hanzi after a quick look in the drawer didn't reveal it right away, I watched him disappear into the dark night air. He left in a small green car; he told me he had borrowed it from a friend. I asked if I could drop the putsi off to him to save him the bother of borrowing the car again, but he said he would return the following week.

When he'd gone, I sat for some time thinking about his visit.

Once I'd finished breakfast, a combination of fresh fruit and yoghurt and a handful of pills the doctor prescribed, I pottered in the garden, breathing in the crisp morning air. I examined pots for shoots from the bulbs Tom had planted the previous October; I couldn't wait for them to flower.

I called in the cat for his breakfast and flung feed to a couple of chickens living in the yard belonging to the farm next door. The pleasant little habits of country living, a million miles away from tooting horns, irritable people clutching mobile phones to their ears, dirty pavements, and kamikaze scooters.

I sighed with happiness and made a mental note to look for the putsi before Tom arrived home. He hadn't rung, but then I supposed he might be recovering from a hangover.

I grinned to myself and returned indoors to shower and dress.

I rarely wore make-up unless I needed to take a trip into the city to meet a friend for lunch or visit galleries; my hair drip-dried now that the weather wasn't so cold. Getting ready in the morning took no more than around twenty minutes. I glanced at the clock, just past nine.

My bedroom was three times larger than the one I had in my city house. Two chests of drawers faced the large double bed; a wardrobe filled one wall, and my dressing table was situated under a large window that looked out onto the lane below. I couldn't remember which of the drawers I'd put the putsi in. I hummed to myself as I pulled open drawers one after the other and sang a little song to a made-up tune of my own: Where did I put the putsi? Put the putsi. Put the putsi – oh, where did the putsi go?

Where had it gone? Blood rushed to my face as I searched the fifth drawer. How would I face Hanzi if I'd lost it? I rummaged through a few old jewellery boxes I had collected over the years, pulling out the secret box I kept under my wardrobe, full of colourful trinkets my grandmother had passed down, along with a few love letters from teenage boyfriends.

I ferreted through now vintage handbags I should have thrifted years ago. I even upturned the linen basket. Surely I couldn't have thrown it away by accident? My heart pounded faster and faster.

I pulled back the Persian rug I used to keep in my sitting room at the previous house, loosened a floorboard, and stared down into the hole where we kept spare cash. We should have fitted a safe, but it was another one of those things we hadn't got around to.

"What are you looking for?" Tom sounded bemused at the sight of me squatting next to the upturned floorboard. "I took the cash to the bank yesterday on my way to Kensington."

I lifted myself off the floor, walked over, and kissed him on the cheek. "I missed you! Did you have a good time?"

He grinned. "Yes, that man's a bad influence; we drank far too much, and he had endless tales to tell about his time in the marines. It was a good night, thanks. How was the face pack and the book?"

I'd completely forgotten my lie. "Oh yes, well, I didn't bother with the face facepack in the end; I just read a bit and got an early night."

He asked again what I'd been looking for.

"The little pouch Vadoma gave me. Every now and then, I like to be in sight of it. It reassures me."

He stared at me a moment, then his brow furrowed. "I can't remember seeing it. I couldn't even tell you what it looks like."

Something made me think that this time it was Tom not telling the truth. He left the room muttering about coffee and how his head ached. I followed him.

"The thing is, Tom, I kept it in my bedside drawer under some photographs, old letters, and other bits and pieces I didn't want to throw away. I never took it out, so I can't for the life of me imagine where it's gone.

He rummaged through the cupboard looking for the cafetière we rarely used. We lazily drank instant coffee unless we had guests.

"You didn't take it, did you?"

"Ah, there it is! What?" He pulled out the cafetière and lifted off the lid.

I patiently repeated my question.

"What? No! What would I want with some old gypsy purse?" He spooned coffee granules into the cafetière, carefully measuring them out. "Do you want a coffee?"

What would Tom have wanted with some old gypsy purse? Good question.

"I've hunted in all the places it could be with no luck; now it's really bothering me."

Tom stopped what he was doing and turned to face me, eyebrows twitching in irritation.

"You are being ridiculous. Just put the past behind you and get on with sending out your paintings, will you? If the damn thing has disappeared, then good riddance!"

He seemed genuinely frustrated with me. Perhaps he did really have a bad headache, or maybe I'd sparked some sort of guilt in him. Silently I left the room, not waiting for my coffee to be poured.

6.

I had to wait until the following week to see Hanzi. I had no contact details for him, so it was up to him to call me. Every day I spent time looking for the putsi. As soon as Tom left the house, I'd be down on the floor squinting under the sofa, emptying plant pots, and searching at the backs of cupboards.

I hadn't mentioned it again to Tom. I didn't dare.

Eventually Hanzi rang my mobile to ask which night he could come. I told him I couldn't find the putsi. "It would be better if you didn't come here. Let's meet at Millie's café like I suggested last time."

Reluctantly Hanzi agreed, and we made a date for the following day at three o'clock.

I arrived early, and Hanzi arrived late. I drank a hot chocolate while I waited, a comforting indulgence including marshmallows and whipped cream to calm my jittery nerves. I debated whether to have homemade shortbread too but decided my hips would only remain as slight as they were if I restrained myself.

The café was small, half a dozen tables at most. I couldn't recognise a single soul. Although I loved living in the country, everyone knew everyone, and occasionally the anonymity of London could serve a purpose well.

Hanzi arrived wearing a dark suit, a white shirt, and no tie—handsomely dangerous— and I thought that if I were thirty years younger, I might have found myself tongue-tied when speaking to him.

The waitress quickly appeared at the table, and Hanzi ordered a tea for himself.

I'd not finished my hot chocolate, and I gestured that I didn't want anything more.

"So you didn't find it?"

"No, I'm sorry, Hanzi, I didn't."

His eyes glimmered, and a thin line of distaste formed on his lips.

"Listen, Hanzi; I think it has been taken. I had it in my bedside drawer for years, and there was no reason to move it. I distinctly recall placing it in the drawer. It's a mystery."

"A mystery perhaps, but there could be a good reason why it has disappeared." He leaned forward, his face so close I could feel his breath. "Jayne, if I tell you something..." His voice trailed away, and he looked around us to see if anyone could overhear.

"You can tell me *anything*."

Our eyes locked. I wanted to help him; I felt bad for the miserable time he'd had as a boy.

"I had an Uncle Ion; he is dead now too. When I was nineteen, he told me a story. I didn't believe it, but it could explain why the Putsi disappeared.

He stirred milk into his tea, taking his time, assessing the colour and finally nodding his approval.

"The thing is, Uncle Ion was— how do you call it? A yarn-spinner. My father Yan warned me not to believe everything he said. In fact, I often doubted him. He was a hard worker but a frequent drinker, and I wondered whether alcohol distorted his memories of events.

Hanzi had my complete attention—his eyes mesmerising, his voice low, his hands gesturing to emphasise his words.

"He told me that in Bunica's putsi there was a ruby. From what Uncle Ion said, a big one. It never got valued, so its worth is something I don't know."

I felt my heartbeat quicken. "So where did the ruby come from?"

"I had another uncle, Great Uncle Luca; he worked a lot on the land. I never knew him. Uncle Ion said he died from tuberculosis during a very harsh winter in Poland. He travelled alone, worked extremely hard, and stashed everything he had in one of those big old-fashioned carpet bags. Numerous tales exist about the wealth he amassed and its potential hiding places." Hanzi laughed. "We live on legends in our culture. As a young boy, I learnt to believe only half what people said. Sometimes less than that."

"But now you think the ruby story might be true?"

"Well, who knows? But it is a mystery how it has disappeared. Things don't just vanish. If there was a valuable ruby in it, someone might have looked inside, seen it and taken it."

"You know. Before meeting your family, I had no faith in clairvoyants and believed the Tarot to be merely a form of witchcraft. But when you all left, I completely reevaluated my life. That and another incident that took place the day you all arrived made me rethink everything."

A small crease between Hanzi's dark brows deepened. His thick dark lashes lowered with interest. "What was the other incident?"

I told him about Ralph.

"It is true; we must follow the path we are given and not give in to those who seek to do us down or give us pain. You did right to stop living the way you were, and I am honoured that my grandmother Bunica played a part in that too."

"I am so happy to see you again, Hanzi. We must find out where the putsi has gone. Tell me the rest of the story."

"Well, as I remember it, Great Uncle Luca had been asked to dig up a large walnut tree on a nobleman's land. He hurt his back while trying to dig it up, and the nobleman took him indoors, fed him, and looked after him until he was well enough to carry on. Such behaviour was apparently unusual in those times. Usually, when such workers showed any signs of weakness, they were left to their own fate. However, this nobleman decided that finding another workman as strong as my uncle would be too much trouble, and Great Uncle Luca was deeply grateful for the nobleman's kindness. When he returned to dig out the roots of the tree, he noticed something glistening brightly in the dark soil— what turned out to be a ruby. Now usually the rule of 'finders keepers' would apply, but because the nobleman had been so kind and because Great Uncle Luca had a powerful sense of loyalty to anyone who gave him work, he handed the ruby in to the nobleman. The nobleman took it and thanked him, and that was the end of it. Great Uncle Luca left when the job was complete and never saw the nobleman again."

"I don't understand. How did the ruby end up in the putsi if that was the case?"

Our mugs were empty, and the waitress hovered hoping to remove them and move us on. New customers had arrived, and she wanted our table. Despite feeling like my bladder was about to burst, I quickly ordered more tea. I excused myself and made a dash for the ladies' toilet.

When I came back, Hanzi had ordered cupcakes for us, adorned with white icing and blue sprinkles. I laughed, "I will go home twice the size; I had a hot chocolate before you came."

Hanzi smiled, showing slightly crooked but very white teeth.

"So go on, how did Great Uncle Luca come to possess the ruby?"

"The nobleman had a servant find him; he'd gone back to Romania to visit his dying father. To this day, no one understands how the servant found him. As a rule we don't leave forwarding addresses. I guess he had a good description and asked people in the surrounding areas where he might have gone. Finding him must have taken a significant amount of time and effort.

Hanzi paused to bite into his cupcake. "So anyway, he found Great Uncle Luca and passed the ruby onto him. The nobleman had left it to him in his will. I can only guess the ruby somehow became part of Bunica's dowry when she married and so ended up with her good luck herbs and such like in the putsi."

I vaguely remembered glancing in the putsi, but all I'd seen was a dirty old stone I'd nearly chucked in the bin. As luck would have it, I felt all the items should remain as they were and popped them back in the drawer. How awful to think I could have thrown away such a precious stone!

I sat awestruck that I had become the guardian for such a hard-earned gem, and now somehow, I had lost it.

7.

When I arrived home, Tom threw his arms around me and planted a loving kiss on my lips.

"I missed you. Where did you disappear to today?"

Here was an opportunity to tell him everything while he was in a good mood. A risk perhaps, but I had a hunch it might lead me to the truth.

I pulled a bottle of wine from the rack. "Want some?"

He nodded, so I unscrewed the cap and poured Rioja into two glasses; I handed one to him and pulled open a cupboard door to grab a bag of cashew nuts, his favourite snack. There was no harm in smoothing the way.

"You wouldn't believe me if I told you." I teased him, pulling up a stool. I breathed in the wine and contemplated how to approach the subject of the putsi.

Tom seemed jovial. He winked and grinned. "Buying me a new laptop—it's my birthday in two weeks— and our anniversary, if I remember correctly."

"Our anniversary? We're not married; how do you calculate an anniversary?" I laughed.

"Never mind." He shrugged. "Where did you go? I called your mobile, but it went straight to voicemail."

I took a deep breath. "I went to meet Hanzi."

"Hanzi?"

His face contorted into confusion.

I didn't speak for a moment. I wanted to see if he would remember the name.

I could see him struggling to piece the distant memories together.

"Wasn't that one of the gypsies who was in your house?"

I nodded and wondered how I should proceed. I decided to tell him about the uncle and the ruby but I didn't mention how Vadoma had murdered her mother. He didn't touch his wine or cashew nuts the whole time I talked, but I took continuous sips of my wine to calm my nerves.

I said all I had to say, and then I fell silent, letting him digest the information.

He lifted his wine glass to his lips. His expression incredulous, he sat back in the chair, folded his arms, and stared at me.

"And you believed that absolute pile of piffle!"

Somehow I knew this might be his response. I didn't say a word. Instead, I nodded.

"You do? Those people invaded your property, your home, took what they wanted, and then fled like thieves in the night. When one of them returns for another go, you extend a warm welcome to him. I can't quite believe it!"

"Hanzi didn't come back for another 'go', as you put it. He came back because he wanted the keepsake from his grandmother. I'm desperate to find it for him; that's why I searched everywhere I could think of. I know it was here in one of the drawers. I can't understand how it just disappeared."

If Tom knew anything about where the putsi had gone, here was his opportunity to come clean. Perhaps he had moved it and forgotten where he put it. Maybe he kept it in a jacket pocket hoping luck would come to him? I couldn't imagine why he might have taken it, but there must be some plausible explanation.

Tom was a sensible, rational man, a dependable man, logical, always planning and thinking and coming up with great ideas. We hadn't had workers in the house for several years; Tom did all the repairs, decorating, and minor building work. He'd worked in construction in his younger years. So no workman or stranger that I knew of had access to our bedroom or house at any time.

I knew it couldn't have been more than a couple of years since I'd seen the putsi.

I tried to think of the last time I'd taken it out to look at it. My brother had been very ill with meningitis; we thought he might die, and one night, when I feared he wouldn't make it through to dawn, I'd taken the putsi out of the drawer and asked it to bring us luck. Please let him survive. We were never particularly close, but the thought of him dying was too terrible to contemplate. Somehow, when daylight arrived, his temperature dropped and the infection started to ease. Slowly he improved back to reasonable health. Of course, I knew that his survival was likely due to the excellent medical care he received, but secretly, I couldn't help but attribute the remarkable turnaround to the putsi.

Tom stared at me. "I feel like I'm being accused of taking the wretched thing!"

"No, it isn't that at all, Tom; don't be ridiculous. I just can't understand how something like that can disappear into thin air. I've always been so careful to keep it safe. And, to be reasonable, I can't think of a good reason why Hanzi shouldn't have his grandmother's purse back. I got the feeling things might be tough for him at the moment and that he needed it."

"Needs the ruby more like. My bet is he only just found out about it, and now he wants to sell it off the moment he sets his grubby little mitts on it. Sentimental value, my foot!"

Tom's attitude worried me. Why would he get so nasty just because Hanzi wanted what truly, in my eyes, was his? "Well, if we can't find it, he can't have it anyway, can he?"

"No, but he knows where we live and has been inside to see what we have, and before you know it, he'll move his lot in when we're out or rob us!" He virtually growled at me. "I can't believe how stupid you have been, Jayne; honestly, I can't!"

"I think you are overreacting. He could have pushed me aside that night and let them in, if that was his intention. And anyway, it wasn't Hanzi's decision to invade my house; he was nothing but a boy at the time. He had to do whatever his parents wanted him to. Yan, his father, was scary!"

"You've really done it now. I ought to ring the police and let them know we are under threat." Tom started to pace the room.

"Tom, that's madness! Hanzi is not a threat; after all, he bought me a cupcake. I realised how absurd I sounded. Was it truly reasonable to believe that someone who can purchase a cake for you is unlikely to intrude into your home?

"Anyway, if I can find the putsi, then I can just give it to him, and he'll leave us alone. It's that simple."

I paused for a moment, barely daring to look at him. Then I breathed out the words as gently as I could: "Did you take it, Tom?"

The wind had got up outside, and I could hear our gate banging. The sudden turbulence outside echoed the unrest within. As I waited for Tom to deny what I had now outwardly suspected him of, I absently thought to myself that there were two kinds of disturbance, each with very different causes.

Long moments passed, and one of our cats scratched at the door; I imagined the chickens fleeing to their coop. I silently wished I could flee there with them. The longer the silence, the more obvious the answer became.

Abruptly Tom stood up, grabbed his glass and the bottle of wine and stormed out of the kitchen.

I spent the rest of the evening upstairs in the bedroom looking up information on my laptop about the ruby that had secretly rested in the putsi for all those years. I found myself particularly interested in the ruby's metaphysical properties. Apparently, the power of the ruby urges the owner to follow their dreams, empowering them to change their world. It certainly seemed to have done that; the fire and passion Tom had put into propelling my career forward had most definitely come into being.

But was Tom right? Did I really believe Hanzi's story? I couldn't understand why he would have reached out to me after all these years, if he didn't believe the story himself.

The wind outside continued to rage; I could hear a carton of some kind tossing around and bashing against fence panels. I shut down the laptop, turned off the desk lamp and sat in darkness by the window. I spotted the empty carton rolling to and fro in the middle of the road. No television noise downstairs suggested that Tom had probably picked up a book or art catalogue to pass time while he sulked.

I couldn't see the point of continuing to search for the putsi. Someone had taken it; that much seemed obvious.

Eventually I tired of watching tree silhouettes dancing frantically against the moody black sky, so I decided to change for bed. My thick cotton pyjamas were a Christmas gift from the ever-practical Olivia.

They were what Tom called "passion killers". I could see what he meant; the bottoms were baggy and misshapen, and the top had large buttons with a protruding flower design on each one. A tight hug would leave indents on his chest. We'd tried it for a laugh. So now they would become my "sulk pyjamas.". When he pleased me, I would wear my sexy silk pyjamas, but when he irritated me, I would threaten him with the sulk pyjamas.

I chuckled to myself as I fastened the top button. In addition to the unappealing design, the colour conspired to repel the most ardent lovers. Deep khaki with shocking pink tulip heads scattered all over. Olivia apparently had a knack for finding such horrors; every year she managed to present nightwear scary enough to frighten even the Bogeyman away.

Amused by my attire, I decided to go downstairs in the hope it would make Tom laugh, thus removing tension over the putsi.

For good measure I slipped on a large pair of owl slippers my brother had bought me several years ago in retaliation for buying him a kipper-shaped tie decorated with dolphins.

Careful not to slip on our well-polished timber staircase. I grasped the handrail and trod quietly. I planned to do a silly dance as I entered the living room; the act surely would dispel Tom's anger with me and cut short the sulk. Years ago this wouldn't have been me, I thought with amusement, the sensible immigration administrator entrenched in my life of dull routine. Trudging blindly towards old age, purposely ignoring what it might be like to have regrets. I shuddered at how my life could have turned out.

As I reached the bottom of the stairs, I heard a voice, low and urgent. It wasn't Tom's. I froze, straining to listen. The voice murmured on, too low to catch the actual words. My heart started to bounce erratically in my chest, and I willed it to stop. I breathed deep and slow, trying to calm myself. No one would be paying a casual call at this time of night. Any of our friends would ring first. They were far too polite and considerate to just show up without warning. Besides, we lived out in the country; it was late. Why would they come now? It had to be bad news. The murmuring voice could belong to the police. I steeled myself and pushed open the living room door.

Tom sat on the floor facing me, his head bent forward, chin resting on knees. His eyes were screwed up and his mouth half open, mid-sentence. A man holding what I took to be a revolver stood next to him.

"Who the hell are you?" My throat went dry, my hands trembled, yet my voice rang out clearly.

The man twisted his neck to look at me. I remembered my attire. Please don't shoot me, I thought, just for looking crazy.

Tom glared at me with such fury I was taken aback. I supposed somehow his current situation had to be my fault. If the man holding the gun had been Hanzi, I would have understood, but this man was a total stranger to me.

The wind outside had reached a gale-force squeal of unnerving sound frequency. My legs became so weak with shock and fear that I collapsed into the nearest armchair.

"What's all this fuss about?"

The man looked back at Tom, cursing under his breath.

Tom hissed, "Shut up, Jayne."

But I didn't want to shut up. The man with the gun didn't spark any recognition in me, and I didn't know this version of Tom either. "Tell me what's going on."

I leaned forward on the chair, readying myself to stand up again.

The man eyed me as if trying to sum up my intent.

I sat back in the chair and crossed my legs. "Who are you?"

Again I didn't get an answer; the man looked at Tom as if expecting him to deliver an explanation. His hair was the colour of ripe apricots — thick and springy beneath a beanie-style hat. I didn't recall seeing his face anywhere before. I noticed his hands were steady and his posture starkly upright. Perhaps he was someone from Tom's naval service days, but he only appeared to be around forty years old, clearly not an old friend. If I'd met him in the street, I might have looked twice; he had presence, and freckles littered his nose in a way that might have appeared friendly in any other situation.

Tom made no attempt to enlighten me. Apparently neither of them wanted to.

I noticed the wine bottle had been emptied; Tom's glass stood alone with just an inch of crimson liquid left. His mobile phone lay next to it, out of my reach; no haphazard grasp at help could be made from such a distance.

What irritated me most was that this ginger man could shoot us both, and I might never know the reason why. Frustration turned my voice into that of a high-pitched school, ma'am— abruptly demanding.

"Right, that's enough; tell me what's going on." I fixed my gaze on the two misbehaving boys in front of me as if I might be about to clip their ears.

Tom threw the man a forbidding look, and all he said was "Duncan" in a pleading manner, but it could just as easily have been sheer annoyance. His anger visibly pulsated in the vein on his neck. I'd never noticed it stand out like that before.

"Duncan?" I repeated it.

No sooner had I said his name than he fled from the room, out through the kitchen, and we listened as he slammed the door shut behind him. It was a forceful closure, but I imagined the wind had some part in flinging it with such a bang.

I jumped out of the chair ready to grab the mobile to call 999, but as I did, Tom screamed, "No!"

I stopped. His head hung between his knees, and his shoulders moved as if he were weeping.

"No? Why not? You, no, actually *we*, have just been threatened in our own home by a man with a gun; the sooner I call the police, the sooner they'll catch him."

I took his reaction as fear and moved again towards the mobile phone.

His voice softened to a whining plea: "No, don't, Jayne; just give me a minute, and I'll tell you what's been going on."

9

Ruby red, the colour of the heart, the colour of love, passion and power – if you can own such a stone with all that it is supposed to bring, surely you have hit the jackpot?

I had spent eighteen years of happiness with a man I had grown to love so deeply and unerringly. If Hanzi hadn't appeared at my exhibition, who knew how much longer this unsullied dream of happiness might have continued?

The Eight of Swords propelled me from the confines of mundane security and thrust me into a realm of boundless possibilities. If that exact card hadn't been flipped face up by Bunica, her spindly withered digits poking it my way, I can only imagine how those eighteen years might have panned out. Of course it wasn't just the Eight of Swords that pointed the way out of my routine reverie. The Ace of Wands sealed the deal with the promise of happier times ahead if I risked it all to follow whatever deep-rooted, half-brained dreams I might have subconsciously harboured.

The cards hadn't shown the arrival of Tom. I'd just taken him as part of my newfound freedom, a bonus in the sliding scale of fortune. Suddenly, anything was possible, and he seemed to make everything that much easier to achieve. Only very lucky or perhaps insensitive people have enough confidence to carry them through life without needing reassurance and support from others. When I used to hear people say, 'Oh, he or she is my rock,' internally I used to ironically laugh to myself; until Tom came along, my rocks had been made of sand.

All that time, and I hadn't known I had another rock in my possession besides Tom. In truth, would it have made any difference if I had known? I guess I would have paid more attention to keeping the putsi safe, and that in turn might have kept my dear Tom safe too.

Why do people do the things they do? I asked myself the same question over and over. Apparently Tom had acted on impulse, and it wasn't out of character for him. Often, he would abruptly alter the entire arrangement of an exhibition. He would bring in oddly shaped boulders to construct a wall, order wines from unfamiliar regions, and come up with a variety of other odd ideas in a sudden burst of inspiration. Of course he would plan lots of things meticulously, but then other things would blindside out of the blue.

This could cause mayhem when deadlines had to be met or costs accounted for. I took it as part of his genius, and as my career went from strength to strength, it was hardly anything for me to worry about. In fact, I could never have achieved all that I did without him.

So when Tom removed the putsi from my drawer while seeking out batteries for his radio, on a sheer impulse, he decided to look inside. There, of course, he found the rough, uncut ruby looking like a dirty stone someone had dragged in under their shoe.

It was quite a big stone, cut and polished; it might be worth quite a bit. He felt hugely excited when he realised what it was, so he decided he could get it cut and set into a ring. He considered proposing marriage just to have a special occasion on which to present it to me. Tom loved more than anything to give gifts, and of course this gift would be particularly special. He racked his brains to think of an affordable place he could get it cut.

The putsi contained only a tiny feather, an acorn, a couple of silver coins, and a small gold ring, likely intended for a child's finger. Tom could have put the putsi back without the stone in it, but instead he chose to hide it in a box in his workshop. He hid it in a place he knew I would never look. I didn't go into his workshop, ever. I respected it as his "man's" cave. He still can't explain why he hid it, apart from the fact that in the back of his mind he may have decided he could use it to present the ruby ring to me. The putsi pouch itself wasn't anything to look at. The leather had been scratched over the years, and the pull cord frayed at the tips, so it was unlikely he would have used it.

Eventually Tom found a jeweller who claimed he could cut and polish the stone. He picked a small backstreet jeweller in the hope they wouldn't ask any questions as to where the stone had come from. When Tom arrived at the small shop, about twice the size of most key cutter kiosks with a workshop at the back not much larger, he felt he could trust the proprietor instantly. The man talked continuously, and all that he said made it sound like he was an expert in his craft. His vast experience and confident manner gave Tom the impression he'd found the perfect person to create the ring. A giant pile of paper orders scattered across a workbench indicated it might take months for the man to cut the ruby into its rightful and most beautiful form. But he thought the wait would be worth it. He made a deposit payment and was required to pay the remaining balance upon collection. This was several weeks before the next exhibition.

Unfortunately, things didn't quite go as planned.

Tom liked to make investments and dabble a little online with stocks and shares. Occasionally he lost a bit of money, but not vast amounts. I knew by his mood that when things hadn't gone so well, he'd get a little snappy.

I remained unfazed; the losses weren't significant, the gains weren't substantial, but everything usually balanced out. Certainly his mood would lift again after a few weeks when he'd done a bit of juggling or stock shares had picked up. Despite trying to make his fortune by gambling in this way, I always felt he had a sensible head on his shoulders and pretty much left him to it. It was a world I didn't understand, so aside from a passing interest, I never interfered. I was too busy creating my epic artworks, and as my reputation grew, the money from these helped keep us solvent.

And then, overnight he lost thousands. It happened at a very unfortunate time, just before my thirtieth exhibition. Determined to ensure the success of the event, he borrowed money from Duncan, his son, whom I was unaware even existed.

I suppose it made it convenient for Tom that I didn't know about Duncan. Anyone I knew might have mentioned the loan to me.

He hoped to repay the money quickly, making sure I would never know about it, but things went from bad to worse, as although the exhibition went well, we had a couple of buyers who let us down and then had to chase several others for payment from previous purchases. Because times were financially difficult for most people, I often let them pay in instalments.

Then Hanzi appeared, which unsettled him further.

Of course now he didn't have enough money to pay for the ruby when it was ready. Hence his behaviour when asked about the Putsi.

Tom never told me about Duncan because he wasn't his biological son. His first wife, who had never been mentioned either, had Duncan from a previous relationship and Tom didn't get on with him. Although he did all the "right" things by adopting the boy as his own and trying to make it work, their relationship never improved. Duncan struggled to accept him, and Tom never warmed to him.

"Of all people, why borrow money from Duncan?"

Tom stared at me for some time when I asked this, as if he needed to fathom the answer for himself.

Eventually he explained that he knew Duncan had a successful business and felt Duncan owed him a little back after he'd tried so hard to be a father to him. Although he hadn't heard from Tom for several years, Duncan was apparently happy to see him again. Despite their uneasy relationship when Duncan was a boy, as a man, he said he understood Tom's situation better and was keen to make amends, rekindle their relationship, and hopefully improve it.

Selfishly, Tom courted him for a while with a view to securing a loan and then decided he'd only contact him again to repay the cash.

He said Duncan gloated about his business and implied Tom hadn't made much of his life.

This wasn't the Tom I knew and loved. He said he feared the jeweller might phone at any time to say the ruby was ready for collection; if he didn't have the money to collect it, what then?

Duncan tried to make contact over and over again, but Tom ignored his calls. Tom thought Duncan wanted the money back, but it turned out Duncan was simply trying to arrange for them to have dinner together.

Eventually Duncan's hurt at being ghosted turned into a fury that boiled over, and he came to the house to confront Tom and demand his money back. Understandably, he felt manipulated and humiliated.

He hadn't counted on a mad lady in tulip pyjamas and owl slippers being there to frighten him off.

It is horribly difficult to find out that someone you trusted for so many years has been driven to do desperate things and, worse than that, caused pain to others in the process. The fact that Tom hadn't told me about his ex-wife and adopted son hurt me deeply.

This wasn't characteristic of the man I'd known all these years.

Still, I guess we are all islands, however close we think we are.

10

Of course I had to tell Hanzi all that had happened.

We met on a rainy afternoon in one of my favourite places: a bandstand in Meadowland Park. Everything looked lushly bright: the trees, the grass, even the moss on the roof. Only snippets of grey sky cut into the variable shades of green.

I had considered bringing Tom along to explain that the ruby was in a jeweller's workshop and that we couldn't retrieve it because the jeweller claimed work had already started and refused to return the deposit. However, I decided against it—Tom had already suffered enough of a brutal tongue-lashing from me.

Perhaps we should have sent Duncan with his toy gun to retrieve the ruby.

Tom had only tried to do things in my best interests, but sometimes all you want is honesty.

When you love someone, whatever happens, you should be able to face it together.

In truth, I wasn't concerned about the money; somehow, I would earn it again. What mattered to me was that Tom hadn't told me about Duncan and that Hanzi's precious family heirloom, the ruby, lay in the hands of a stranger.

Despite Duncan entering my house with a fake gun, I felt sympathy for the emotional turmoil he had been in to be pushed to do something so extreme.

What a mess!

When I arrived, Hanzi stood with his back to me, gazing out at the rain-soaked park.

The swings had been abandoned. A crazy black labrador chased its tail while the owner frantically called to him. Round and round, it ran, thrilled with its disobedience.

Hanzi listened to me intently as I gushed through what I had to tell him. The ruby really did exist.

"So the story was true." His tone was dreamlike.

In the man, I could still see the boy taking an imaginary drink from my goblet.

Relieved that he didn't appear angry or demand that I get it back immediately, I smiled.

"When I can eventually afford to pay the remainder, I'll make sure it comes to you, Hanzi. I feel dreadful about the whole situation. At least I still have the putsi; Tom returned it to me."

With a wistful smile on his face, Hanzi turned to face me and asked, "What would I want with an engagement ring? I am already a married man."

I shrugged. "You could always give it to your wife. Or if you have a daughter one day, pass it on as part of her dowry."

He gently kicked at a spur of stray wood jutting out of the bandstand floor. "So you would rather not marry Tom?"

It was a question that caught me off guard. I was more preoccupied with how to raise the money to get the ruby back, so I didn't have an answer right away.

"I can't think about that now." I snapped. Then I said more softly, "Anyway, I thought you needed the ruby or at least wanted the putsi?"

"I wanted to know if the story was true, see the ruby, and touch it." He paused. "But it's not all that important." He laughed. "Perhaps you could arrange to leave it to me in your will."

I smiled. The rain had eased off a little, and the sky lightened to a white-grey nothingness. The crisp air carried the scent of freshly cut grass. I inhaled deeply. "I'd like to meet your family."

Hanzi gazed out into the park, frowning a little. It took him some time to answer.

"I don't want them to know how we used to live, not my wife, not my boys. No one ever mentions it in the family. Only one of my brothers still lives in other people's houses, but I don't agree with it. We are better than that."

"So why did your mother and father live like that, moving from house to house?"

Hanzi stared at me a moment as if trying to sum up what my response might be.

"They came from a horribly poor place. Some Roma are impoverished, while others are affluent. We were the poor— very poor. My father did not have the brains or energy, or even the luck, to get us out of poverty. When they heard that life would be easier here, they left our community. Our people have always travelled, so it made sense for them to come to England. They heard the government might give us money for not working, that people had great homes, and no one had to struggle like we did in our muddy streets with little to eat and no proper healthcare. An illness that would have been easier to treat elsewhere claimed the life of one of my younger brothers.

When I saw what happened with Bunica and my parents, I knew I had to find a better way to live. We went back home after Tata died in the street brawl. Vadoma was ill from drinking, and my older sisters insisted we return to Romania. I wasn't far into my teens, and my mother insisted I marry Borca. She had connections with a wealthy community in Buzescu. I met her cousins and older brothers, who bought and sold cars and farm machinery, and I began to work with them. It wasn't easy, but gradually I earned enough for us to move away and stand on our own feet, as you say here.

Borca is better educated than me; she taught me to read and write, and she is a good woman, if a little argumentative." He stopped and grinned. "If you could see the house I live in now, you wouldn't believe it. Buzescu is like our version of Beverly Hills; we want for nothing."

He paused.

"Hanzi, I am glad you managed to do so well. I really am."

I put out a hand to squeeze his arm, and he shrugged.

"I was lucky to have a way out presented to me; otherwise maybe I would have tried to come back here and find work, you know, do things properly."

"So you came all the way back here just to find the putsi?"

"I suppose I wanted to tie some ends up. Also, I had a little business to do here. I wanted to find out what had happened to you and if the putsi was still safe. It seemed I arrived at a— how should I say it—an intriguing moment in your life."

I smiled, a little ruefully.

"I wish you could see what I was wearing when I burst in on Duncan and Tom's argument; you would laugh your head off!"

"But you have done so well; you have achieved so much. Your art is truly wonderful, and I like to think our disturbance in your life—your home— ended up freeing you to do something you really wanted to do. Not that what you were doing wasn't good." He added quickly.

"Sometimes we need to be shocked out of our complacency. A lot of my success is up to Tom, but it took your grandmother and her tarot cards to really make me reconsider my life and decide to do something different; otherwise, I suppose I might have unhappily plodded on with a life that didn't fulfil me. It seems we both owe Bunica for our change of direction."

Hanzi smiled a big, beaming smile. "Oh yes, her and the Eight of Swords."

"Will you walk back with me? I'm getting cold now."

Arm in arm, we walked across the wet green grass.

"So what's next, Hanzi?"

He stopped a moment and looked at me.

"Well, perhaps when you get the ruby back, we will find out."

THE END

Thank You for Reading!

If you enjoyed these stories, I'd be incredibly grateful if you could take a moment to leave a review.

Your feedback not only helps other readers discover the book, but also supports me as an author to keep creating more stories to share with you.

A few words go a long way - thank you for your support.

You can leave a review at Amazon and/or at Goodreads

Follow Petra Kidd on Instagram & Facebook,

www.ingramcontent.com/pod-product-compliance
Lightning Source LLC
Chambersburg PA
CBHW051500050726
47593CB00005B/2163